THE
DUNWO]
KILLINGS

Christopher D Pearce

For Laura, the lighter part of myself,
And for Diana,
To whom my love goes without saying.

CONTENTS

ACKNOWLEDGMENTS

There are a number of people I would be remiss if I did not thank for their assistance in the creation of this, the first published novella of mine. Primarily, I would like to thank Laura, the light in my darkness and the better, kinder part of myself. Thank you for being the first to read my first draft and supporting me through the whole hair-pulling process of getting it to this point. Also to Chris, who read with enthusiasm and offered advice and critiques when Dunworth was in its early stages. To Ellie, I say thanks for your excitement at each chapter you read, it really spurred me. Thank you as well to Ziito who has encouraged me to work and not give up writing even when I have found myself on the verge of frisbeeing my computer off the balcony. Of course Livi as well, who helped me find my voice in so many ways when I thought it lost.

  And to Diana, my grandmother, my true guardian, and my sister, Lucy, who both have watched me build my worlds from my childhood and supported what began as an aimless hobby.

  I love you all very much.

I

The car stopped, sharp and sudden. At either side did hedges rise and loom unkempt, curling inwards and nearly touching overhead, directly above the middle of the road, to form a tunnel. That effect blocked what little light the late evening could provide.

The road, for it was one despite how scarcely deserving of the name it was, was wrenched apart in places by cracks and potholes. That part of the country was too far out of the way for the local council to really care at all, much less do anything about the state of it. The long stretch of country lane led only to two farms and nothing else worth mentioning. Thus when the car pulled to a halt along that darkened stretch it seemed a most curious place indeed.

I sat up in the passenger seat. I had been staring unblinking at the wild hedgerows as they passed by, my eyes flickering over unseen images as the car sped along. I had been reflecting, not all that tentatively, upon the last few weeks of my life. Now my calm monotony had been disturbed and I was jarred quite riotously back to the present all at once.

Before the car and beyond the headlights was very little. The unhappy darkness drank up the light a few metres ahead and the road disappeared into that gaping maw. I stared into it, through the mire of evening and deeper still. I found it oddly terrifying knowing that not a single thing scarier than myself, the driver, or even the car in which we drove stared back.

The driver had been going slowly, as one should along such dubious lanes, but now that they had stopped entirely I knew I should feel quite ill at ease.

I definitely should have felt that way.

Over the grumbling purr of the engine there was nothing. No owls hooting in the night, no bugs in the bushes, no foxes screeching as the are wont to do. It was as though not a thing lived in the world anymore, and that thought was serene in its quiet horror. I did feel quite exposed then, protected though I was by the chassis of the vehicle.

'Why have we stopped?' I asked at last. I had not realised quite how long it had been since I had spoken a word and my voice sounded hoarse. Looking around for a water bottle proved fruitless. During the journey I had already finished several and my belly had been aching as it swolled with urine. Still I felt unsated.

'There are frogs crossing the road, some voles too I think.' The driver told me. 'I don't want to kill them.' The driver sat there, tapping a finger upon the wheel and chewing another quite impatiently.

After a short time I too had grown impatient.

'Just drive. It's freezing out here. I would rather live than worry about some *voles* and freeze to death.' I was tired and aching. We had driven all the way from the next town over where I had left the train. It seemed to have taken hours, so remote was our destination. Such was the lonesome nature of isolated west-country towns, and this was hardly something I had missed at all. The old car was not comfortable and I certainly was in no mood to be talking. I did not much like thinking either and had done my best to sleep through the journey.

The driver tutted but did not move the car. I think I would have preferred him to counter my curt command.

I wrapped my coat which I had been using as a blanket about myself all the more and huddled against the window, irked to say the least. I had not seen my aunt in years, nor my cousins, not since well before my mother's death. I could scarcely remember what the farm even looked like, but I knew there would be a bed and silence which, at that time, was all I desired.

Soon enough, I felt the car begin to creep forward again. The little creatures must have started to move out of the way. I peeled back my eyelids, unaware that I had even been sleeping. Perhaps I had only been there a moment, dancing that line between consciousness and the easier, less horribly tangible otherworld. I stared into the night, considering the vast emptiness of it.

And the night stared back.

Something huge shifted just beyond the window. There in the devouring blackness, two pinpricks of light reflected what little illumination there was to be had in that abandoned place. For only a moment the moonlight illuminated strands of shaggy black hair and something wet glistening by the window. Steam pooled on the glass and spread out like ink in water.

I did not yell out. Perhaps anyone else might have been afraid. I didn't even want to move in case whatever it was, whatever stared in from the shrouding night at me suddenly lunged. The driver would startle and likely cause an accident in panic. Mostly, I think I managed to somehow reason to myself that this vision was only that and that alone.

The thing beyond the window stepped closer and I could see then the face of a huge black hound, its eyes wide and hungry, teeth bared and tongue lolling free from its jaws.

The driver went on, never having noticed the beast just feet away. I was also paid no mind.

For the rest of the journey I watched the wing mirror. Would that dog chase us, I wondered? But every time I looked back there was nothing there chasing us but for the night.

It took another hour from then to arrive at the farm.

The road we had been driving down had forked suddenly, for the first time in perhaps five miles. Along the narrower path we had gone, the northward road. The thicket of trees about us had grown more dense initially, replacing the obstructing hedges through which my driver had taken a leisurely amble. Even the sallow light of the moon found filtering through that canopy a challenge not worth the effort. Suffice to say I was irritated and tired by the time we arrived at the farm belonging to the Dunworth family, Crawbeth.

It was an exceptionally old house, one that had been in the Dunworth family for generations and had been the primary source of income for them throughout that time. To look upon it then, even in the dark as we rolled up the drive, peeling through the thicket, one would not have guessed thusly.

I remembered Crawbeth House as a brilliant white building that would gleam like diamond refracting the summer sun. Then, as we pulled up the long driveway before the front of the house, it was grey like rot about a wound. Even in the dark I could see the paint chipping away from it, particularly where the ivy had begun to eat at the corners of the house. It was larger than I remembered, though I guessed that this was due to my age and not that Aunt Ruth had made any extensions to the four-walled home.

No disappointment at the disparity between my memory and the decrepit reality did I feel. Perhaps someone else might have, but I had always been told that I had been a painfully stoic person, even as a child. I knew that the joyous days of childhood would be painted in the brilliant hues of a holy ecstasy, but these were falsehoods. Despite what horrors might have been inflicted upon us as youths, we would more often than not see things like a family home with a wilfully naive optimism and admiration. The state of Crawbeth House came as no gut-dropping surprise to me.

Despite the headlights I could not see beyond the house. I knew there to be stables and a large barn with pens for goats and pigs and the like but where they were I could not as yet recall, suspended in the mystery of the early hours as I was. I knew there was a garden around the back of the house which led onto an allotment and then downhill into several fields and then the woods which separated the Dunworths' home from that of their neighbours'. Most all of the surrounding land belonged to Aunt Ruth and my late uncle Harvey and I was sure that someone would take me around the area come the morrow though I knew not if I had the energy or bother.

The driver switched off the engine and all at once the deafening silence of the countryside drank me down. My eyes could not permeate the dark and I stared through it to where I knew the house to be. I had forgotten how entire such an experience of such blackness was. To not be able to see one's own hand before your very own eyes but to be able to see so many stars, thousands of them like white paint splattered across tarmac, it was quite extraordinary.

A light split the night and the front door opened. In comparison the hallway was too bright to define anything that may have been within but for the approaching silhouette of a tall woman.

Aunt Ruth stood unshod in the door, a nightgown wrapped about her slender frame. I could not as of yet see her face and she became no clearer as I removed myself from the car and thanked the driver.

'Jacob,' She said, her voice thick with sleep, 'hurry in, love, it'll rain soon.' I could not tell why she thought so for the sky was still afire with starlight, nor was there any thickness to the air that one might find towards the end of a glorious summer. Not heeding her advice I kept my pace and came to the door after only a few moments. I stepped into the porch and was swallowed by the warm light. Ruth waved goodbye to the driver without invitation for respite from the long drive back.

I dropped my bag by the door where there were only six pairs of shoes placed neatly upon a rack. It was only a small bag for I had so few possessions in the world. Never had I been a particularly sentimental child and the impermanence of the recent circumstances of my life had only served to accentuate this trait.

Before I had fully slipped out of my coat to hang it upon one of the pegs by the door, Aunt Ruth had turned me about to face her and wrapped her arms around me. She held me there in that suffocating embrace for a long while through much of which I did not reciprocate, startled at the spontaneity, as I was. It must have been quite the awkward pose to see, my coat still hanging onto only one of my shoulders. She ran a long, delicate hand over my hair and held me tight.

After a time I had had all that I could bear of this and lightly pushed myself away from her. I saw that she was crying. She held my cheeks in her hands and looked down at me, rubbing away tears that were not there with her thumb.

'Ah, you poor child,' Ruth stood up straight and dabbed at her own tears with a sleeve of her nightgown. I forgotten the lilting tinge of her accent. My mother had long since lost that by the time she had died. 'What a sorry lot you've been given. If I'd have only known what a sod that dad of yours would be I'd have taken you in myself, I swear I would've!'

I removed my coat. I was not certain how to respond to that. We began to walk down the hallway together towards the kitchen.

The inside of the house was no real improvement from the without. Faded textured wallpaper like veins fell away in strips and every surface was covered in thin layers of dust. Pictures which lined the walls in broken frames were hung at jaunty and accidental angles. The telephone table was missing a leg and yet somehow remained upright, though I was sure it would presently collapse were it to be disturbed at all.

At the end of the hallway was the kitchen. Instantly as we stepped within I remembered myself as a child sitting there at the head of the table. I would stroke the old cat, Fred, listening to his rhythmic lovely purring and feeling his body vibrate under the soft fur. I remember that, doing so, I could feel my fingertips dance over his protruding ribs which I did feel with wonder. It was astounding to my curious and nearly infantile mind how fragile he felt. We would sit like that for hours paying no attention to whatever the adults spoke of.

I suppose I found it curious if anything to think that, of those four, my mother, my father, Aunt Ruth and Uncle Harvey, two were dead and only Ruth remained. Though it had been little under a decade before I was last at Crawbeth, to me it felt an entire lifetime.

Ruth told me to sit and I obeyed. I sat in the same spot I used to. This time there was no Fred. Like as not the cat had long ago run away to live in the wild, or had just died.

Ruth went to a cupboard above the sink and poured two glasses of whiskey. I could not tell if she was still crying. I suppose I did not really understand what she was crying for. These things had not happened to her. Why would she sob for the incidents of my own life when even I did not? Presently, it seemed almost self-absorbed and preformative of her to do so.

She set the glass down in front of me, retrieved the bottle and sat as well. The table was massive, bigger even than I remembered it being. It was large enough, in all likelihood, to seat twelve people.

'A dog chased us along the road.' I told her. I think I said it because I did not know what else I wanted to say. I did not want to say anything, but clearly I was being forced into interaction then. To be forcibly interactive, I felt, was the nature of families, though I had never been a part of one but for my own, and such was certainly *their* nature.

'A dog?' She asked, stopping her glass before it got to her mouth.

'A dog.'

'Chased you?' She wiped her face which was only a little wet from tears now with the back of her sleeve.

'Yes.'

'Along the road?' She seemed dull witted after all these years. I suppose I never really remembered her being overly intelligent but this conversation was taxing.

'Yes, Ruth. A dog. A big black shaggy dog chased the car I was in along the road. It kept chasing us and then it wasn't anymore.' I didn't mean to sound quite as rude as I did but I did not apologise.

'Gosh,' she said. She finally took a sip of her drink. 'I don't know any dogs like that. The Pedersons have terriers. Are you sure it wasn't a terrier?'

I wanted to hit her. Perhaps then she would stop, like a screaming alarm clock at the crack of dawn.

'Yes, Ruth,' I said slowly, 'I'm sure that the big black shaggy dog that chased the car along the road was not a number of terriers.' *Idiot.*

'Couldn't have been Adah, she's been asleep by the fire all night.'

'You *still* have Adah?' I was genuinely shocked. That dog must have been nearly twenty years old. I never remember having seen her as a pup, even when, growing up, my mother, father and I lived in the village near Crawbeth House. The last I remember she had that tinge of grey which dogs get about their snouts when they are starting to get old and her eyes were turning milky and crystalline.

'Oh, of course!' Ruth chuckled. 'As healthy as an ox that one. Sometimes I think she might outlive me.'

Beyond the window the night had ravaged and consumed all the world. It was as though the panes of glass had been painted black.

'I'm very tired, Aunt Ruth. Could you show me to my room?'

She looked up at me with big sad eyes. She had the same eyes as my mother. I did not match her gaze for long.

'I'm sure you are, love.' Reaching then across the table, she squeezed my hand and gave me a sympathetic smile and a look which asked if I was okay. I was not. I was tired. I didn't have the capacity for conversation with Aunt Ruth in the small hours of the morning. I just wanted to sleep. My brain would turn off and that would be quite lovely until I woke up again. 'What an awful, awful time you've had.' I did not know what to do with my face. Should I thank her? 'Come on,' she drank the last of her whiskey in one go. Mine was untouched. 'Come, I'll show you to your room.'

My room was a small 'L' shape at the front of the house, overlooking the drive through which I had entered the property. Within, there was very little furniture and while everything was covered with the same thick layer of dust that the rest of the house was it somehow seemed much cleaner. There was an odd cold and damp smell like earth and water, somehow.

The bed, a small single fit for my size, though only just, was placed in the corner of the room with the only window overseeing its middle. Pink floral bed sheets were tightly laid across, the bed clearly having been made only hours before my arrival. By the bed was a table of no more than a square foot and twice that in height. The wood had gained that odd glaze of blackening grease which one might see upon unpolished furniture of a certain age. Across the room, directly before me as I entered, was a dresser over which a mirror hung, one which was now all but opaque with time.

Even the air was stale. I dare not open the window, however, as the night I knew had a chill to it and I did fear the beast which had followed me for so long. In my fatigue-manifested delirium, I found myself wondering if it could follow my scent there to Crawbeth. Would it find a way to enter the house and tear me asunder?

'Thank you, Ruth.' I said, setting down my bag. I sat on the edge of the bed and stared at her, waiting for her to leave, offering no grateful smile.

However, despite my obvious coldness, she did not leave for a moment longer. She stood there looking at me in the same way she had at the table. Those sad eyes with a sympathetic smile. Too long did she linger for my liking.

'Goodnight, Jacob,' she said, turning the corner to leave the room. 'I'm so sorry he did that to you, you know. I hope the bastard dies in that cell.'

'Thank you, Ruth. Goodnight.' I said, because I did not know what else to say. It was a curiously morbid show of camaraderie and support, one I thought there to be few appropriate reactions.

She did not close the door as she left. I went to it and closed it, turning the light off and allowing that vacuum to permeate me.

I felt something spur me into the night like a pull at my heart.

Neither clothes nor a true consciousness did I wrap myself in for warmth. I needed them not for there was no warmth in my acts thus none belonged upon my supreme personage.

Naked as a babe would, I came into the world again. Everything was shapes and colours and as unrecognisable and nonsensical to me as it had been upon that day of my birth.

My feet did split upon the uneven roads and the punishing stones which had been strewn across them as though in an effort on behalf of the country itself to deter me from my dread task. I washed the dirtied and bloody flesh of my haunches in the stream which divided me from my quarry. Refreshing though it was, I found the chill of it miserable compared to the gushing ambrosia within which I had hitherto bathed myself. Even the very thought of what was to come stirred an excitement within me I dare say bordered upon erotica.

Through the night there I peeled and prowled, my footfalls silent so as to not alert the world around me to my coming. It saddens me to admit of my failure in this, a small aspect of my task, for a bird did hear as I stepped upon an unnoticed branch which snapped like a bone. That dastardly fiend took flight there and called through the treetops. In that entire shroud of the hour I could not see but I cursed it inwardly. That hate going unrepressed made me sick.

At last! Free of the hindering trees and there before me, inviting and warm, a light and the dull tones and snores of it, calling me like the smell of the burrow to the coney.

Brazenly I walked through the courtyard, that place stinking of all sorts of foulness and fodder having intermingled most repulsively. A light snapped on and the world came alive again though dead still as it was. No sign of life came from the house and thus I halted my pace not. To do so would mean a slower conclusion to my task and thus increase the chance of discovery.

The barn was not secure and I slipped in as easily as a fox into a henhouse. Hardly even did I disturb the doors upon their aged and screeching hinges. With my presence then known a stirring could be heard all across that hollow tin domicile. They all groaned in fear and backed away from me, colliding with one another as they did so. My silhouette cast out over the ground and I dare say its length and ominous gait did bring unease even to my own dark heart.

It was not a random choice, nor one preconceived. I had to wait for one to offer itself to me, thus sparing the others. The slither of light in which I stood was not quite enough to illuminate all corners of the room and thus many of those beasts did remain hidden to me as they wailed and roared in confusion and fear.

All but for one. A great fat red one. The eyes which I could see, and I dare so those which I could not, were wide and wild and afraid. As they rightfully should be. Her eyes were inviting and casual, lazy and tired, so, so tired. She just wanted to rest.

I then obliged.

What horror I inflicted upon her was something most intimate. It was a unity between the two of us, a bond between our eyes unparallelled in any interaction I had with those of my own flock.

Each motion as I severed the link of body and soul and wrenched herself away from the earthly vessel was equally delicate as it was artistic and vicious. My body throbbed as I stared down at the viscera, sinew, and organs which were caked upon mine own flesh. I sucked these from the space under my fingernails after I was done, revelling in the taste of it.

That, and how easily I would get away with it.

II

Aunt Ruth woke me for breakfast the next morning with three sharp knocks upon my door.

I removed one of the two pillows she had left for me from over my head and sat up, sore from the unfamiliar bed. The house stank of eggs and bacon.

My journey the previous evening had exhausted me and I was still quite stiff of movement. I rolled over with a groan, listening to the sounds of my aunt and cousins making their way down the stairs for their morning meal. One walked with a steady, nonchalant and effortless pace whilst the other lumbered, every other footfall a thump on the landing then breaking suddenly into a mad dash down the stairs. Such a cacophonous rancour did the latter cause that I believed for a moment that someone might have been injured. My concern was so minuscule that it did not yet inspire me to remove myself from under the floral blanket.

The curtains in the room Ruth had given me were flimsy and melancholy things. Now that the sunlight fell through them I could see dozens of holes marring their already hideous cascade. I poked at one such perforation, my finger punching straight through and onto the glass which was cold and wet with the dew of a country morn.

Having removed myself from the bed, I dressed leisurely. It was not that I was overly concerned about my appearance. Indeed, I had stopped caring a while ago as was evident by my greasy hair and sordid complexion. As an adolescent, these were things all but wholly unavoidable, or so I had reasoned. Simply I did not wish to make any haste to the table where my cousins would already be waiting to greet me with curious and pitiful stares.

The house was old and a chill bit through its bones like an insidious flow of water through a weathered pipe. I pulled on a jumper over my t-shirt and stared into the mirror. My shoulders were slumped and I made no effort to right them. Not from my recent awakening were my eyelids so low but rather from the disenchantment of where I then found myself.

This had not been my plan.

Only when Aunt Ruth called me again did I leave the room, closing the door behind me.

The kitchen seemed far more familiar during the day, particularly then thanks to the addition of my cousins, Chuck and Ellis. The old dog, Adah, slept in the corner by the side room and breathed so shallowly and infrequently that I was not entirely convinced that she *was* still alive as Ruth had claimed the evening prior.

With my ongoing morbid circumstances, I suppose I had never thought of myself as an average adolescent, but when confronted with Charlotte Dunworth and Ellis Harold Dunworth I felt the comparison favoured me, in spite of all my cold and unsmiling strangeness.

'*At least now we can bond over dead parents,*' I thought terribly. Of course I said nothing. I barely greeted them as I took my seat, but they both stared at me as though I were some curiosity at a fete, or even some predator which was poised to lash out.

Charlotte, or Chuck as we all called her, was the eldest of the three of us. The nickname I could not quite remember the origin of. It had just been how we had all always known her. Perhaps Uncle Harvey had been the originator of the moniker. After all, Chuck had always been far closer with her father than she ever had been with Aunt Ruth. I wondered if as much was still the case by then.

She had changed much in the years since last I had seen her, more a young woman than the filthy little girl with whom I had chased the sheep in the Pederson's field. Her face had hollowed and hardened into a girlish shadow of her late father's. Dark hair hung to her shoulders in a wild unhappy mess, one which I found Ruth's acceptance of most curious. I suppose she might have been pretty if she had been a boy. Lips curled at the side in a perpetual and perhaps unintentional snarl which was recent. I did not think of her as having a happy face.

That latter trait was one she shared with her brother, Ellis. He was near enough at an age with myself, but the two of us could not have been further apart in every aspect. I do not remember much of Ellis from our childhoods for it was so few and far between that he was allowed to integrate with the rest of the family. My mother once told me that when he was born, Ellis did not cry and they all believed him to be a stillbirth. It had been a difficult pregnancy and that tragedy was one which Ruth and Harvey had prepared themselves for. But he did breathe. He wriggled and thrashed and stared into his mother's eyes when she held him, never blinking.

Ellis' nightmarish eccentricity had extended into his later years, such was plain enough to see as I sat then across from him. He stared at me from under his brow. His skin was dirty and stained and bruised. Clumps of his hair were missing but to my laymen's eye the cause was not alopecia but rather a violence, such was plain by the rawness of the skin. It was a habit he had fostered in his early years and had never apparently kicked. I remembered my father saying once that Ruth and Harvey should have known how much of a challenge

Ellis would have been. He had feverently believed that a difficult pregnancy begat a difficult child.

I did not really know how much stock I put to his words. Besides, I had been born from a caesarian, so I did not know how his philosophy had applied to me, his only child.

'Good morning, Chuck,' I said, knowing my attempt at a smile was feeble enough.

'Mornin' Jacob,' She nodded. She sipped her tea. It had not been an impolite greeting, but one which the confidence and familiarity of I had found somewhat charming.

'Good morning, Ellis,' I said to be polite, knowing he would not respond. His eyes flickered to me and he might have grumbled something. Just as easily it may have been a growl.

'How did you sleep, love?' Ruth asked. She still wore the same gown she had the previous evening. The pan before her spat and hissed viciously. Already had she snatched her hand away from it several times. 'I'm making eggs, bacon, sausage, black pudding, got some beans on the go, there's gonna be toast and, well, the works! Oh, shit, I should have asked if there's anything you don't eat.'

'I don't care,' I said flatly, crueller than I had intended, 'I'll eat whatever you give me, Ruth.' I did not want to eat. I could not remember when last I had wanted to, but I did so regardless purely for the necessity of it.

Ruth set our plates out before us. Chuck ate none of the meat but Ruth had put it before her nevertheless. Ellis only ate meat and, juxtaposing Chuck's own meal, nothing else was upon his plate. He did not use cutlery. Ruth was humming a cheerful tune the whole time. I pushed the food around with my fork and nibbled only at the odd mouthful.

The phone rang and Ruth stopped humming. Her brow furrowed and I even thought I saw her jaw clench. Neither did Ellis respond well to the sudden interruption to the uncomfortable familial peace.

'Well, who's that?' She asked none of us. 'Yes?' She said curtly, putting the landline to her ear. Whoever was on the other end said a few words to her and Ruth disappeared quickly into the side room. Adah raised her head and looked to my aunt with milky eyes as she passed, sniffed the air, and lay back down, apparently ultimately deciding whatever the matter was it was little of her concern.

'Some sorry luck we've got, eh?' Chuck said, pushing the plate away from her and in front of Ellis. He greedily snatched at the plate and ate the meat which was left.

'Huh?' I grunted, putting down my own fork which had only some dry bread on its end. 'What d'ya mean?'

'Them lot.' She nodded towards the room where Ruth spoke in sobs to the caller. 'Mum's a loon, your dad's a diddler, and your mum...'

'Yes, thanks.' I said, cutting her off. Was she trying to be cruel? Either that or she was just a callous idiot, I supposed. 'I'd rather not talk about it.'

'None of us would, Jacob,' she scoffed, folding her arms over her chest and rocking on her chair's hind legs, 'and that's why times like this are so uncomfortable. You *do* want to talk about it, I can see it itching away in there.' She wiggled a finger at me, right between my eyes. 'You found your mum, I hear. I bet that was awful.'

Her form flashed up before me. The white bathroom splattered red. The sink was cracked from where her head had bounced off the basin. She lay face down, the towel tangled up in her mess of limbs which seemed to suddenly have no bones. She looked not at all posed like that, but rather had fallen in the chaos of a real accident.

'No, it was not my favourite thing.' I said because I had to. I put another piece of egg in my mouth and hoped she would just shut up.

'Mum was in hysterics of course. It was only a couple years after dad died,' that seemed to stop her for a moment, but she quickly collected herself. 'I said we should take you in, of course, didn't want you going to your dad's because I knew he was a fuck. Sorry about that.'

'You didn't do anything.' *Just stop talking.*

'But we could have.' I wasn't sure if she had caught my meaning. 'You should have *killed* him, Jacob.' She said, echoing her mother's sentiment from the previous evening.

Before either of us said anything else Ruth returned to the kitchen. She steadied herself on the table and placed the landline there, not in its cradle. Her face was red and wet and her eyes were puffy. In a flurry of motion and words broken by sobs she went to the sink. She poured herself a glass of water and drank it from a shaky hand.

'Goodness,' she said, gasping after several long gulps, 'that was Stanley Pederson. Some animal got into their barn last night and savaged one of the cows. Oh, gosh.' She gasped and pressed the back of her hand against her forehead quite melodramatically. 'Oh, gosh. Must have been a badger, or something. He's coming over later. Mr Pederson is clearing away the body and Alice is moving the rest of the herd to the other barn. Stanley will be over later once he's helped them. Going to have a drink with us, I expect.' She breathed deeply through her nose. Her knuckles were white where she gripped the edge of the sink. 'Oh!' Ruth exclaimed excitedly and I was surprised at her sudden change. 'Oh, Jacob! You'll get to meet Stanley. He's a darling, you'll *love* him.'

Ellis grumbled something. He pushed away his plate which was clean but for greasy finger marks. He hopped off his chair and ambled away out of the kitchen, slumped and angry like some brute. Adah stood on unsure legs and followed after him.

'I've got to lay down,' Ruth said, her mood suddenly darkening again. She walked to follow her son out of the door but stopped as she passed Chuck. 'Don't disturb me, Charlotte. You can look after your brother. *Don't* wake me. Don't wake me until Stanley gets here.' Her words were somewhere between a command and a desperate plea.

Ruth gripped her daughter's shoulder and Chuck shrugged her off. My aunt disappeared out the door and made such a racket going up the stairs that I thought she might have fallen down it over and over again.

'Cunt.' Chuck hissed, rubbing her shoulder as she rolled it.

Stanley Pederson was the only son of the Pederson family, who were themselves the only neighbours to the Dunworths. He was a handsome fellow, only a few years my elder, already boasting the shadow of a beard on his heavy jaw. His hands were large and rough, scarred all across, doubtless from years of work on the farm. He wore a checked shirt which fit him well and displayed a strong form which had been hidden upon his arrival under a jumper and heavy jacket.

He sat across from me, smiling and talking with Aunt Ruth who I had not seen for most all of the day. After her sudden retirement at breakfast she had stayed hidden in her room for several hours. On occasion I would hear her suddenly wail upstairs or the sound of something breaking, but never did I pay it much mind. Such reminded me all too much of my mother's own episodes which I then began to realise might be some inherited and invisible malady.

I had seen nothing of Ellis all day until the late afternoon when I noticed him standing at the end of the garden. It was not a big garden and what there was of it had long since overgrown. Thanks to the rain it had also flourished nicely in the warm season and it was there I saw Ellis watching bugs and birds dance in the air with a fascination of one half his age.

'He once ate a vole.' Chuck had told me when she saw me watching his innocence. 'We tried sending him to school in the village but he didn't do well, as you'd expect. He was violent to teachers and other kids, smashed things, ripped up books. Never said a word of course. One day, just after dad died, he just lost it. Stabbed a kid in the mouth with a pencil, charged outside and bit the head off a vole. Just his teeth.' She smirked, looking then out to him as I had been moments before. 'Extraordinary.'

It was curious that the focus of the story had not been the assault on a child, but I too quickly moved passed the fact and thought little of it.

I did not know how to be tactful.

'What's the matter with him?' I asked.

Chuck shrugged. She was covered in paint. That's what she had been doing all day, sitting in one of the side rooms and just covering canvas after canvas with paint. I watched her through the door for a while as she was sketching out the face of a dog which might have been Adah, but I had grown bored and went to read in a field. There was not much else to do at Crawbeth.

'Nothing medical,' she said, 'he hasn't any sort of disorder or anything, nothing any doctor can diagnose anyway. He's just... a bit odd. Mum would never admit it, of course, but I once found some leaflets about an asylum up in the moors. I imagine she was thinking about putting him there. Either that or going herself. She's always been afraid of him, you know?'

I did not know, but I could certainly understand.

Ellis had stood there for hours and hours and it was only in the late afternoon when the rain had begun to threaten that I had thought it a good idea to bring him inside.

He had stood in that same spot the whole time. Never once had he turned his body from when I had noticed him earlier with Chuck, but rather his head dashed about at the flutter of each little creature as it passed.

'Ellis?' I called from the back door. 'Ellis, I think you should come in.' His head jolted in my direction without turning and I knew I would have to go to him.

As I had been about to take a step out the door to him, putting on some wellington boots which had been left without, Chuck's hand which was still wet with paint pulled me back.

'Leave him.' She insisted. 'He's quite alright. He knows when to come in. Besides,' she looked over the reddening sky, 'nothing out there is going to hurt Ellis.'

I had thought it strange but did not have the energy to protest, nor did I care at all. Instead I took myself to the kitchen where I would sit and gather my thoughts. I did that and only that for some time. I do not rightly know how long passed as I sat there but when I emerged from my own psyche the room was utterly black.

Not for long did it remain thus before a knocking came upon the front door and Ruth suddenly flitted into the kitchen as though she had been waiting just at the bottom of the stairs by the back door for the sound.

When Stanley had come into the kitchen Ruth had gone right to him. He looked glum but there was something about the lazy loping gait with which he entered that made him seem not melancholy but rather more akin to a bashful pup approaching a new owner.

I had been surprised at his visage and how quite agreeable I had found it. He gave my hand a firm shake and smiled politely.

The three of us had sat there for some time, drinking the rest of Ruth's whiskey and then some more which Stanley had brought with him. He smoked tobacco which he rolled into cigarettes himself and after a few drinks Ruth had asked him to make one for her too.

She did not like it and left it in the ashtray, but after another drink continued to puff idly on it throughout the rest of the evening.

At any given opportunity Ruth would stroke his knee or run her thumb over his cheek and his olive complexion would redden with excitement. I did not know if they thought they were being subtle or if they did not mind displaying their blatant affair before my eyes which were those of a newcomer. Surely such a romance would have raised a few eyebrows in the village and not to mention with Stanley's parents. Ruth was near twice his age and by the way she pawed at him one might have thought her a love-struck schoolgirl.

It was plain enough to understand why. He was certainly handsome and thus far I had not heard anything either irksome nor hateful from him. People such as him, I thought, were easily attractive, without complication or malice to their being, just kind and gentle. It was as though he had never known any hate, never known anything but joy.

He had told us the details of the killing the evening before once his lips had become looser and, indeed, to hear him tell it it had been quite a grizzly affair.

'See, I'm not so certain it *was* a badger or a fox like Dad thinks.' He said, slurring somewhat. I was captivated, but by now Ruth had a glassy look over her hungry eyes. 'I don't know, don't quote me on anything, but I saw the poor girl. It didn't look to me like she'd been attacked with teeth and claws. More seemed like a knife. Those weren't scratches like she'd been fighting, they were stab wounds, I think. Like I say, don't quote me, don't go to the papers with that. Ah, hell, I'm leathered. Don't listen to me.'

I nodded, waiting for him to go on. He was quite finished though.

'Do your parents think the same?' I asked.

'Don't know.' Stanley shrugged, taking a sip of his drink and running his thumb along Ruth's wrist, 'Dad was pretty pissed off about it so I don't think he was looking too close and mum just wanted him to get rid of her before she stank up the place.'

'How compassionate.' Ruth slurred. She sounded like my mother.

Stanley offered a snort of laughter. I mirrored it.

'Well, you know how they are. All business, I guess.' He started rolling another cigarette. 'Mum said, and I guess I agree, that at least it was only a cow.'

'What do you mean by that?' I asked. I felt disappointed, but in a way which I would not express.

'Well, horrible things happen to animals all the time,' he said, putting the tobacco into the paper, 'Maybe they're used to it, even if they don't know, maybe there's something within them which expects it, like how we are innately scared of spiders. I don't know. At least it wasn't one of us.'

'So,' I said slowly, 'you think they're built to suffer and we aren't?' My tone wasn't pointed or accusatory, only investigative.

Stanley took a sip of his drink and looked me over, perhaps trying to assess the intention behind my question. 'Not in the same way, no.' He replied after a while. 'I don't know they have the same level of mind as we do to know true suffering.'

'Perhaps we shouldn't compare levels of suffering at all. Suffering is suffering. Physical pain is suffering, just because a cow can not muse on its misfortune doesn't make the immediate pain of what happens to them any less tangible for themselves. Does that make sense?'

Stanley did not say anything else immediately, but stopped his glass just before he pressed it to his lips, mulling over what I had just said.

Ruth got up and stumbled away having mumbled something I didn't quite catch about the toilet.

'So, what's your story, Jacob?' Stanley asked, licking the paper to stick it down then smoothing the whole thing out between his fingers. 'You staying here long or just down for the weekend?'

Unlike the Dunworths I detected no hint of malicious agenda in his tone. He was simply curious about my presence and meant not to antagonise. It was refreshing, but regardless I found his curiosity more intrusive than anything else.

I decided to scare him then. It would be a way of asserting my dominance over him. To do so, I told him the truth. I felt like an alpha of a pack, my teeth to an underling's throat.

'My mother died a couple of years ago.' I said flatly. I did not take my eyes off him as he lit the little cigarette with a match. His lovely eyes softened. He exhaled.

'I'm sorry to hear that, mate,' He passed me the cigarette across the large table and I took it without hesitation, 'was it peaceful, at least?'

'She cracked her head off the bathroom sink and died next to the toilet.' I told him, blowing a ploom of smoke back at him. He seemed surprised at my candour and I realised then how long it had been since I had actually engaged in conversation and found myself somewhat enjoying it. Naturally, my playful malice would not serve to devise an enjoyment which he could reciprocate.

The alcohol had lowered my guard and I found myself desperately scrambling to take the words back in even as they so readily fell from me. As much as I was enjoying seeing him stumble over himself quite awkwardly, the memory of the incident was causing me to feel quite uneasy. 'She was a drunk, you see. I don't really remember a time when she wasn't. I heard her crashing around that night, trying to take a shower before bed or something equally as stupid. Of course I was used to her making all sorts of noises at any hour so I didn't go to check on her until the morning when I went to brush my teeth for school.'

No sorrow then embraced me, no fury. There was no tightening within my throat, trying to stifle a choking sob. None of that happened at all.

Perhaps he was surprised at how coolly I told the story, but such could have only been expected from one who had been forced to live and relive the same scene over and over dozens of times to anyone who asked and thrust a badge in their face.

'Fuck,' he said, taking the cigarette back off me and inhaling desperately. 'Fuck, that's brutal. I'm sorry, that must have been terrible.'

'Yes, it must have been. It must have been terrible for her to die that way.' I said quickly. *Stop talking.*

'So, you moved here after that? Didn't you say it was a couple of years ago?'

'I tried my best to fight it but in the end my dad took me in. I didn't want to go. We had not seen each other in years since my mother kicked him out.' *Stop fucking talking.* 'I was there for only a few weeks before he started...' That was where I tripped up, 'you know what? I've said enough. I don't want to put a downer on everything, maybe I'll just go to bed.'

'You got somewhere to be tomorrow?' Stanley asked as I stood up.

His eyes glinted. He was holding onto tears. Sweet boy.

'Don't worry about dampening the mood, Jacob,' he reached out and patted my hand. His palms were just as rough as I thought they would be. 'It's not like we were on particularly cheery topics anyway.'

'Thank you, Stanley, but I feel I've embarrassed myself and I would like to be alone with my thoughts.' I lied, I was just sick of being around people. I patted his hand and stepped away from the table.

'Well, goodnight then, Jacob. It was nice to meet you.' He only then let go of my hand, 'I will see you soon, mate.'

Stopping in the doorway, I locked eyes with him for a moment during which Ruth returned to the room and did not seem to notice my impending departure.

'Yes.' I agreed, 'I think so too.'

In that same stream from the evening prior I washed my naked body under the moon. I let the water fold itself again and again over my feet which moved not even as they began to burn from that black cold.

The previous evening had been so exhilarating and I felt anew. In the fields beyond the domicile wherein my latest piece had been left to be found I had breathed deep of the night air as I felt the carnage and viscera harden and seal into my own being. I had stood there in the nothing of the night and caressed myself all over. My soul rolled over and over with the pleasure of it and I had wailed in ecstasy knowing my calls of heaven would not be heard by any.

I felt content and sated for the first time in recent memory. I felt the muscles of the white horse bounding over clouds between my thighs. I felt the harrowing immensity of my action. I felt the danger of discovery and its twinned excitement. I felt the rolling orgasm shatter my resolve in the evening.

Again! Again! I wanted more.

But no. Not so suddenly. Not so soon.

I would have to savour this one for now.

This beautiful and pristine completion of another grand piece.

Just as I thought thusly did a fox scuttle up by me. It had not seen me where I rose from the water like some dread naiad. She offered herself up to me, drinking luxuriantly from the water wherein I washed off my hateful self.

With a violent and sudden sound did I pounce at her, grabbing the vixen by her scruff and shoving her face down into the stream which I could hardly see.

She thrashed against me but her strength was meagre and mine was plenty.

After the briefest of instances, her struggle stopped and I shuddered again with joy, coiling my dirty hands into her rough orange fur.

III

Stanley and Ruth had not been shy about their love making. It had gone on from the small hours until little after the sun had returned to herald the morning. At times it had sounded like Ruth was dying and I wondered if I should go on in and help her.

I had lay there in the bed upon the pink sheets staring at the unmoving ceiling. The house was old and the sound of each moan and giggle and screech annihilated the silence which would otherwise exist so perfectly there around me. It was as though they were in the room with me and the implied intrusion made me nauseous.

The alcohol was hot in my gut and I needed water. I needed to piss. Maybe I was going to be sick. Maybe I wanted to be sick. Maybe that would help. Maybe.

Downstairs the lights had been left on. I stood there by the sink trying to force the water down all at once. In the countryside, the water was delicious and already my hands had never felt softer or cleaner. Anyone who said water tasted no different in the city did not drink enough of it.

I had sobered somewhat over the hours I had been motionless in my new bed. By then I was quite agitated and only wanted to be outside again, but cautious of disturbing the rest of the house any more than Ruth and Stanley already were, I made no move for the door.

The following noon I stood in the back garden, pulling on the wellington boots slowly. I felt quite awful by then and had managed only a few hours of sleep. Ruth had made me force some dry toast down myself when I had refused her offer of breakfast. Stanley had apparently left shortly after sunrise, though why she bothered to tell me as much I could not have been sure. Like as not she was just excited to have someone new to talk to.

As was her want, Chuck called to me from the backdoor as I was making my way out of the garden and down the path which led to the fields at the back of the house. She was wearing faded jeans and a cream woollen jumper which appeared much too large for her skinny frame. She sorely needed to brush her hair. It was easy for me to criticise her, though my own hair was in sore need of a wash.

'Where you going, then?' She asked me, the twang of her accent irksome to my hungover self. Chuck had quickened her pace to catch me up though I walked at a laborious pace and had yet to make it more than two dozen yards away.

'I was going for a walk down the fields,' I told her, not caring a damn if I sounded at all harsh. I wanted to be alone and I was already growing bored of the intrusive Dunworths. 'I *had* thought to be alone and collect my thoughts.'

By then we walked at a pace with one another. Chuck was nearly skipping along next to me. Her hands were stained with paint.

'Bollocks to that!' She laughed. 'I'll come with you. I'll take you down to a lovely spot.'

'Chuck, I think I would rather be alone, I'm afraid.' I protested, closing my eyes against the bright sun.

'No, you wouldn't. C'mon, Jake, let's go.'

No one had called me Jake since my mother died.

I hadn't the energy to protest further and walked with her. We crossed into the next field which rose somewhat to obstruct the view of the horizon. At the top, the view was quite lovely and showed just how remote Crawbeth House actually was. It looked out over valleys and fields which stretched for miles around like a great patchwork quilt of all shades of green. Cows in the distance were faintly hovering dots. Birds erupted from trees like an explosion. I could even see the blue sky once again, so hidden had Crawbeth been by a grim shroud of both cloud and tree.

We walked for well over an hour. The whole time Chuck chatted away and after a time I began to feel somewhat more alive and before long found myself engaging with her. She told me she had been painting for a few years now and felt that she had gotten quite good at it. Mostly she liked to do images of the rooms at home or the animals but occasionally she would paint Ellis. He liked her company, she thought, and he could certainly sit still long enough without moving.

She did not like to paint Ruth. So often she would move around too much, disappear from the room without leave or talk incessantly. Occasionally she would get angry at nothing at all and once even tore apart several pieces she had worked on the weeks before.

It became more apparent to me over that time with Chuck how little she liked her mother, though she never explicitly said so. I remembered there being a coldness between the two of them even when we were younger. Chuck had always been close with her father, Harvey, more than her mother.

There was a longing about her which was plain enough to see. A separation of self, as though part of her personality had been torn away or locked up.

'Wait a second!' Chuck suddenly declared, cutting herself off mid sentence. I had only been half attentive to whatever she had been talking about but the sudden change startled me nonetheless. 'We need to turn here. I recognise that stump.'

I followed her as she made her way to the left of our path. Thus far we had travelled true along our invisible path. Were we to turn back upon ourselves we would arrive eventually at the back door of Crawbeth House.

We walked then towards a treeline which divided us from the next field over. My footing was not as sure as hers and on numerous occasions did I slip and nearly injure myself in some unseen hole left by some dastardly badger.

It did not take much longer after that for us to arrive at our intended destination. Quickly I recalled it.

Before us was a deep pool into which fed several streams. It was not the prettiest sight, muddied were the waters by a recent downpour, but the sound of the water trickling in over rocks and fallen branches I found soothing besides. The serenity had caused Chuck to stop talking for which I was also grateful.

She knelt down with her legs folded under her, not giving a damn about muddying her jeans. She smiled. I did not kneel down to join her.

'It's lovely here, isn't it? I sit here for hours sometimes. Mum wouldn't come down this far and of course she'd never let Ellis come with me so it's a quiet little retreat that's just for me.' She pulled out a pack of cigarettes from her back pocket which I did not know she had. The pack was battered up quite severely, barely holding together but for the plastic wrapping about it. She lit one with a match and then flicked the little bit of wood into the pool. She offered me one and I accepted, matching her every moment thereafter.

We stayed like that for a little while, smoking our cigarettes and looking at the small forest around us. There were no sounds of animals, only the gushing water into the pool. Chuck lay down after a while, one leg resting over the other and humming away quite happily.

I stood at the edge of the little mound overlooking the pool. I could see my reflection in that murky water, distorted somewhat by the small waterfall nearby. Watching myself smoke was odd in that way, the sinking of my cheeks as I pulled in and the reflection of the smoke obscuring myself from myself even more.

'Were you ever told how my dad died?' Chuck asked me after a little while.

It had been nice not saying anything with her. She only ever seemed to want to talk about death, about morbid things. I suppose it was natural at that age to be curious about everything, particularly the macabre and taboo which he had hitherto been shielded against. It was only recently in our lives which we had become aware of things like death and sex and the meaning of real violence, what was forbidden and why. Of course it was natural to think terrible things and want to say them aloud just to gauge a reaction and explore those topics.

I just did not want to say anything. I did not ever want to say anything.

'Yes. Well, no. I know that he...' I could not find the words to be polite. Hell, Chuck had not bothered being polite at all so why should I? 'I know that he killed himself. I just don't know how.'

Chuck smirked and blew smoke into the air above her where it disappeared into the trees.

'He shot himself with his shotgun downstairs. I paint in that room now. I guess it's weird but I suppose I feel close to him there.'

'It is a bit weird.'

'Thanks.' she laughed. There were three breaths of silence.

'Why did he do it?' I asked.

Chuck propped herself up on her elbows and shrugged.

'Not too sure really. He didn't leave a note or anything. We had had a fight that evening, him and me, but it wasn't anything to kill yourself over.' She laughed once, then fell suddenly silent for only a few seconds. She seemed to be considering the muddy pool. 'Well, I suppose it was, maybe. I don't know, do I? Why does anyone do anything? He must have been miserable for a while, I guess. That's why you kill yourself isn't it? I don't know, I've never done it.'

'That's a terrible thing to say.' I told her. My cigarette had gone out and I held it in my hand. I was not sure what to do with the end. I did not want some foolish creature to come along and eat it, not knowing any better, and die.

'Oh, bollocks,' she waved a hand at me.

'What was the fight about?'

'Well, Officer, if you must know I watched him skin a deer.' I made a face, one she echoed. 'Yeah, exactly. I was twelve and dad thought that was old enough for me to go hunting with him. Obviously, I wasn't all too aware yet of what it was to hunt and *actually* kill something, so I was quite excited. I didn't much like the killing as it was but when dad brought the poor thing home with us and I watched him skinning it in that back room where I paint,' she made a noise, 'it was all a bit much. He carved up some steaks and said we were having venison.

'I kicked up a right old fuss about it. I wasn't eating that! I had been staring at its eye the whole way home waiting for some flicker of life. That was the day I really understood what death was.

'Dad and I yelled and hollered at each other in the kitchen calling each other all sorts of things. He said it was just an animal and that's what they were for. I told him he was a monster for wanting to do all that to a thing, regardless if it wasn't a person. I called him some other things and he smacked me in the mouth. That's when I lost my last two milk teeth, mind you.

'He took himself away without another word and mum tried to calm me down. She put peas on my face and put me in front of the T.V. I had it up quite loud so I didn't really know what the gunshot was when it happened, I suppose. Mum came in and told me there had been an accident. The two of us and Ellis went to bed and she held us there for a while. I was pretty scared because Dad wasn't there in the bed with us.

'I guess I didn't really know what had happened until I woke up alone later. Mum's room was flashing, there was an ambulance outside. I went downstairs and the paramedics stopped me. The lady took me back to Mum's room and just told me that there had been some accident, again.'

Chuck stopped there and I suddenly felt quite rotten for having asked her anything at all. She stared up into the canopy of trees above and then swore before lighting another cigarette. That time she did not offer me one.

'That's terrible. I'm sorry.' I said because I knew I had to.

'Pah, fuck it,' she said. 'It's not like he killed himself anyway. I'm just surprised she got away with it.'

I did not say anything else to that. What was the appropriate response when your cousin accuses your aunt of murder? My hands I kept busy by tearing apart the filter of the cigarette. The stink of it was revolting, but it occupied me.

Aunt Ruth was certainly eccentric, perhaps suffering from some troubles, but I had not thought her a murderer. Really, I do not think I accepted Chuck's insight and I was not all that sure if she did either. Like as not she was looking for someone to blame for Uncle Harvey's death and could not believe that that person might partially be her own self.

'Say,' Chuck said, sitting up suddenly, apparently having forgotten the whole sordid thing, 'what's that over there?' She nodded over towards where one of the streams fell from by a tree into the sunken pool. That small waterfall cascaded down from a pile of rocks and debris. Upon it something curious rested. It was not a branch nor was it a stone nor a pile of mulch.

Chuck stood up and we walked around the perimeter of the pool's elevated edge to get a better look. 'Oh, fuck,' she said when we finally fully percieved what lay before us.

A fox lay dead against the side of the stream. Its whole body was soaking wet as though it had been submerged for a while. The back of its neck was bald and raw as though it had lost a fight with something larger than itself.

'Oh, no,' I said, 'it must have got in a fight and come to the water to clean its wound.'

'Why would it need water for that?' Chuck chided my ignorance. She was slowly getting closer to it as though expecting it to jump back up at her. 'They're quite pretty in the daylight, aren't there?'

'Uh...'

'Well, obviously not like *this*. I just mean the colour of her coat in the light. Oh, never mind. Should we bury her?'

'Why would we do that?'

'Feels like the right thing to do.'

'Did you know her?'

'Sod off. Whatever.'

'We may as well let nature take its course. Something will come along for her by the end of the day, I'm sure.'

'That isn't very sensitive.' Chuck objected, folding her arms in front of her.

In response I only shrugged.

I could not stop looking at it. Chuck was right. She *was* quite pretty in the daylight.

I stalked my home for hours. That horrid thing inside me was chomping at the bit. It was hardly sated from what I had offered already.

The rooms and hallways I left in darkness so as not to aggravate my already anxious mind. I wanted to go outside again. I wanted to run under the moon and hunt for something again, to feel that gush of gore and that rolling orgasm again. I wanted to scream into the night again. I wanted to feel something again, and that I could only achieve with my heinous artwork.

The act of the previous evening had hardly counted, no. It was not such a display, not such a masterpiece as the first. It would not be found by anyone who cared.

I growled and rumbled like a storm. Each movement was jittery and unsure and thunderous at once. Why was I denying myself? What harm was another so soon? I was very good at it.

Before I knew it I was outside again. Running naked along the dirt roads I felt my hands graze on the harsh ground. I sniffed at the air and roared again and felt lighter as the moonlight swallowed down my throat. I could smell the musk which fell from birds' feathers, the scat left tactfully by the nocturnals. I could practically taste it.

For miles and miles I ran, ignoring the pain in my feet just as my prey would until I saw the light of a house up ahead. It was only one shining through a window but against the unswaying night it was as the sun.

I prowled up to it, slowing my approach as I neared the property for fear of activating any security lights. Somebody sat inside, long asleep before a flickering television. I paid them no mind as they were not to my taste. Slowly, I slithered towards the window, passing the low fence with a seamless ease.

Within the home I saw no signs of life besides that slumbering old woman. There were no toys or little beds on the floor or anything of the like.

Giving up, I crawled around the side of the house on all fours and grinned hungrily at what I heard.

Four, no, five, hens had become alert to my presence. They flapped and moaned and fought over one another to be further away from me. They had no loyalty to one another but only wanted to escape from their wire cage.

Every movement was imperceivable as I approached, slow and meticulous and precise. My tongue lolled hungrily, a glob of saliva dripping from its tip. They could only see my form as it swelled in the night. Perhaps the glint of my eyes and even those I did not blink.

It was all too easy.

IV

I awoke in cold piss and the hot rancid smell of it.

Maybe I had been having a nightmare, but whatever it had been was receding from memory hastily.

Quickly I jumped out of the bed and took off my clothes. I piled them all onto the bed and stripped that as well. I stood there in the dark, holding the sodden and sordid bundle, unsure what my next move was.

This had happened numerous times when I had lived with my mother but back then it had rarely been an issue. I knew where the washing machine was. I knew how to operate it. Standing there in the silence of Crawbeth House in the darkness of the small hours I was at a complete loss.

Where did they keep the sheets?

What next?

Shit.

This had not happened in years. I felt a panic coming over me then but as my breathing quickened the stink of my own urine filled my nose from the bundle I held against my chest. I was furious. I wanted to scream.

As I crept from the bedroom and made my way downstairs, I found that I was aware of every slight sound. The house screamed and moaned at my presence and in my attempted subterfuge those sounds were deafening. The utter darkness hindered my vision and the bundle in my hands allowed me not to feel my way through the house. My journey down the stairs was a slow and precarious one. Every second made my teeth grind against each other.

The side room off of the kitchen was one of the few I had left to explore and common sense told me that this was where a washing machine might be. As I approached the kitchen door, walking adjacent to the stairs, I stopped, realising suddenly my error.

Leaving the soiled sheets in the machine overnight would not serve for surely Ruth would see them before I and question us all. Equally I could not put them through a wash cycle and risk waking up the house at such a ridiculous hour. That left me with only one choice.

Dropping the bundle by the back door I hastened back to my room. Calm had settled over me by then as my plan had formulated and rationally I knew that no one would query my wandering the house at this hour, likely they would assume I had gone for a glass of water. Lying was something I was becoming all too proficient at.

In my room I pulled on some jeans and a jumper. I did not waste time with socks. I hurried silently back down the stairs like a burglar and unlatched the back door slowly so as to not hear the booming crack of the lock. The sheets I grabbed again before spilling into the back garden.

The world was black.

Now that I was outside of the house I did not feel the necessity to slow and dampen my movements. I rushed through the garden and onto the path where Chuck had caught up to me earlier that day before making a left at the end of the drive instead of crossing into the field and went on down the country lane.

Down that road I walked with my secret held tight to my breast, still smelling its foulness. The whole situation was repugnant yet I felt no embarrassment whatsoever for it was unfortunately all too familiar.

My own breathing was louder than a summer storm. I found myself getting lost in its jagged rhythm as I walked on and on and on and on. When I no longer could see the shadowy silhouette of Crawbeth House upon turning my shoulder I decided to walk some more. My legs were sore by then but still my heart was quickened, not simply from the threat of discovery but realising then the repercussions of my impulsive decision to walk so far. Eventually, I would have to head back.

Finally, I was satisfied. I tied the bundle up and stepped off the road into the muddy patch of grass at the side of that dirt road. Reaching over into the hedge I stuffed it deep inside. The branches scratched thorns against my arms and pulled threads from my jumper. Regardless of the pain of tearing skin I persisted, hissing through my teeth and swearing loudly.

This made sense. Country roads always had refuse and odd, shapeless objects discarded by them. Anyone passing might think the bundle, if they saw it at all, to be some roadkill or a discarded coat. Before long they would become filthy and animals would drag them away to make their nests out of the soiled evidence of my shame and all would be forgotten. No one had to know. The next day, when I woke up, I would ask Ruth where the washing machine was and have her show me how to use it. The query would simply be disguised as simple curiosity at my new surroundings. It would all be fine. No one would ever have to know.

But I was not alone. The realisation came upon me as suddenly as the light did. At first it was just a pale white illumination of my task and then it fixed upon me. My hands were visible but the bundle was barely there anymore.

Thinking quickly, I fell to my knees and lay there for a moment in the muck and the mire on the side of the road. After a moment I pushed myself up, swearing loudly. Whomever was passing would think I had fallen whilst taking a piss on the side of the road.

'Jacob?' A voice called.

The light was too bright and shining directly at me it was all I could see. I put my hand out to cover the light and made out the tall, athletic frame of Stanley Pederson approaching me in the dark. 'Jacob, are you alright?'

'I fell,' I said, not at all relieved to see him. I would have preferred a murderer. Perhaps then I would not have been so embarrassed. At least in the dark he could not see my reddening complexion. 'I was taking a piss and I fell in the mud.'

'Damn.' He said. He was close enough now that I could see him just about. The light from the bright white torch was all the illumination we had and at the angle he held it did it formed odd shadows and shapes across his otherwise handsome face. 'That's shit.'

'No, it's mud.' I said.

'What are you doing out here?' He asked, not appreciating or not understanding my jape, 'You're about a mile from the house.'

'I couldn't sleep.' The lie came easily.

Stanley shone the torch at me enough to see me. He smiled softly at the state of my jumper. My arms were all scratched up and I could feel that my face was much the same.

He reached out in the dark and touched my face. His rough thumb ran along a cut under my eye. I did not wince but he made a face as though I had.

'You shouldn't be out this early, mate. C'mon, I'm heading your way, we can walk together.' He said, nodding down the path.

'Nah,' I shrugged, trying to wipe some of the mud off myself to little avail, 'I'll wait for the bus.'

At that he laughed. I smiled and followed after him.

We walked at a pace together though Stanley stood maybe six inches taller than I. I was a middling height for my age and Stanley, in a legal sense, was a grown man. His legs were long but I walked with a natural haste anyway as I always had. Often I had been told I always seemed to be charging towards something, or fleeing from something else. To me it seemed such could be the case for just about anyone.

As we walked, the light wobbled on the path as though Stanley's grip was unsure. Like many other aspects of his character I found this to be quite endearing.

'What are you doing anyway, mate?' I asked. I did not like how the colloquialism fit my mouth but I said it anyway. 'Coming to rob us?'

'Yeah, I thought I'd make off with some of Chuck's paintings, sell 'em as my own and make it rich in the city. But as I've told you, I suppose you can get in on it with me, if you'd like.'

'Nah.'

'No, I told Ruth I'd come over today and give her a hand with some things.' I could hear the smile in his voice. 'Plus, with what happened last night I thought I best come over early and make sure everything was alright.'

'What happened last night?'

'Ah, shit,' he said. He rustled for something in his pocket. After a second I felt his hand touch mine and he slipped one of his rolled-up cigarettes into my fingers. 'Pretty nasty, something got into a lady's chicken coop and tore the things to shreds. Quite vicious apparently, but she'd slept through the whole thing. Passed out in front of the telly, mind, but you'd think she'd have heard something, wouldn't you?' Having finished lighting his own whilst he spoke, he passed the lighter to me in a similar manner he had the cigarette. I fumbled for it deliberately. His fingers were not nearly as cold as my own.

'Shit,' I said in a similar manner he had. 'Maybe it's that killer of farmyard animals you were talking about?'

He made a face.

'Shut it, you.' Everything Stanley said seemed to be playful with me.

'What time is it anyway?' I asked.

'Maybe four-thirty by now.'

'Bit early to be skulking around isn't it? The house is gonna be quiet for a few hours yet.'

'Well, *you're* up, aren't you?' Again, I could hear his expression, one I mirror once he had turned to me. 'Ruth gave me a key.' He explained.

'Makes sense.'

'Ah,' He said slowly, cautiously, 'so you know then?'

'Of course,' I laughed at him, 'and Chuck knows. I don't know what Ellis knows about anything, but I'm sure he knows.'

'Oh,' he sounded bashful but I thought it best to not study his face too obviously, too closely, despite the utter darkness 'I didn't know.'

'I assume Ruth doesn't either.'

'Nah,'

'Probably best to keep it that way, then.' While Chuck thought her mother to be a killer, a sentiment I was still not fully behind (though I had spent much of dinner that evening studying every word and movement of Ruth's,) I did not think it wise to confront her with knowledge of her apparently secret affair with the neighbour boy. Already in the few days in which I had been living with the Dunworth family I had seen near-violent fluctuations in Ruth's behaviour and mood. She was proving unpredictable, and though I feared her not, I did think it prudent to do my best to discourage these personal discrepancies.

We walked together silently for a few moments.

'It's not really anything to me, I reckon,' He told me, 'but I think she loves me. It's all a bit odd, you know. Her husband only died a couple of years back. I knew Mr Dunworth. I didn't like him all that much but I knew him. He was friends with my dad. Well, not friends, but they were friend*ly*. Thing is, we've been at it for a while now, me and Ruth, but I'm seeing this girl in town, Hannah. She's pretty nice, as well. Of course neither of them know about the other. I don't reckon Ruth wouldn't take kindly to that sort of thing.'

'Are you going to be my new uncle out of awkwardness, Stanley?' I asked him.

'Don't be silly, Jacob,' he laughed, 'Chuck's only a bit under two years younger than me. That'd be weird.'

'Yeah,' I agreed. 'That would be weird.'

Just then he stopped.

He reached out and grabbed my hand to stop me continuing along the path. I snatched my hand away more violently than I had intended. Stanley tried again and grabbed the sleeve of my muddy jumper. Turning about to look at him, in the dim glare of the light bouncing back on his face from the torch I saw terror.

The light shone right down the road and I followed its path. Something hulked there in the darkness. Its form was odious, one rear leg twisted behind it and its body hunched low. It steadied itself with a foreleg on the ground and the other curled up against its body. As our movements and the clumsy sounds which came with them had ceased I could hear its low, guttural breathing like the score of some nightmare. The thing before us sounded as though it had recently been strangled, so wretched and pitiful was that sound.

Immediately I thought of that phantom dog which had chased the car upon my initial arrival at Crawbeth House.. However, as Stanley's light stopped shaking (largely thanks to him now grasping the torch with both hands) I saw it was a skinny, pale thing, with no hair at all. It twitched in an erratic way as though disturbed by a swarm of flies. From it I could hear a hideous, even pathetic growl that came from deep in its throat. I could hear that even from where Stanley and I lingered perhaps twenty metres away.

Genuine shock overcame me and I stumbled back a few steps, grabbing onto Stanley's arm. Of course, I knew what this nightmare creature was, but he gave me quite the start anyway.

'Take off your coat, Stanley,' I said quietly. He did not protest. His mouth hung slack and his eyes were wide on the wraith in our path which had most horrid skin the colour of moonlight. I took the coat from him and told him to hold the light steady.

Slowly and calmly I approached Ellis where he crouched naked in the road. That white flesh was covered all over with goosebumps. It was a mild night but I did not know how long he had been outside. Presumably, he followed me out when I had fled the house to hide my shame earlier on. I must have forgotten to close the door behind me.

'Ellis,' I called out through the dark. His head shot in my direction. There was fresh blood dripping down his face from his scalp where he had recently pulled out more hair. Timid and bulging eyes did not meet my own. 'You're cold, Ellis. Take Stanley's coat and we'll go home, get you into bed, yeah?' My voice was as soft as it should have been.

Some syllables tittered from his chattering teeth at me as I approached. They sounded not like anything overly disagreeable so I put the coat around him. He righted himself as much as he could, though his shivering would remain quite fierce for a while yet.

'What the hell?' Stanley hissed in disbelief. He was quite afraid, quite small there in the dark with us. Though he was older than I, I certainly saw much of a frightened child in him just then.

I did not know if I should put my arm around my cousin to keep him warm and close or if this would startle him. Ideally I would have asked Stanley to carry him home so that he did not hurt his feet any more on the treacherous lane, but I thought it best to not disturb him any more than necessary. What I already knew of Ellis was strange and unpredictable, I need not tempt any further curious occurrences that evening. The sooner much of it was forgotten and we were all back at Crawbeth, the better.

The rest of the walk back to Crawbeth was a slow one. Stanley and I did not talk much more the whole way. Occasionally, Ellis would bark out in pain as he stepped on a rock and I understood then why he had been ambling along the road in such an animalistic manner. When he did so I would offer some reassuring words but besides those none of us said a thing. Plainly enough, Stanley was suddenly quite afraid of the dark lane.

We came upon the drive leading up to the back garden after a long while. The sky was turning the colour of a day-old bruise and I was by then quite tired. Mostly I was worried that I would sleep for the rest of the day and become unintentionally nocturnal.

Stanley and I escorted Ellis upstairs to his room. My own bedroom door was still closed but Ruth's was not, at least not fully. From within the kitchen I could hear her voice rattling on and on. She spoke softly but I do not think that anyone else was present.

This disembodied conversation filled me with a sudden anger for it reminded me quite irksomely of my mother, Ruth's sister. So often would I hear similar mutterings coming from behind closed doors, though my mother's own utterances were thickened by her lewd drunkenness. So often I had wondered if she had thought she was actually speaking to anyone at all, or if she did it just for the simple fact that she knew that it annoyed me.

Ellis' room was terribly small. There was room enough for his single bed and not much else. A chest of drawers stood by the door and on top sat a picture of the Dunworths. They were all smiling in a very real way, sitting on some beach somewhere. It did not seem like the people I had come to know again over the last few days.

Nothing hung from the white walls. There were no books or toys anywhere to be seen. The curtains were colourless and every surface was laden with a thickened layer of dust. All the room stank of mould and body odour, coalescing in the damp, nearly putrid air. Moonlight fell in through the window and tiny particles danced upon its beams.

Stanley put him into bed and pulled the sheets up over him. Ellis still shivered but his growling had lessened into a drowsy whisper. We stood there in silence looking down at him for a moment. I suppose Stanley was waiting for me to do something but I was just listening. Ellis whispered into his hands which were cupped before him but I was not sure he was speaking any language at all.

We left the room and Stanley shut the door slowly and quietly behind us. We stared at each other for a moment and I did not know what to do besides that.

To my surprise, he hugged me. He pulled me into him with one arm and wrapped them both around my shoulders, resting his head against mine. He was quite cold and yet somehow smelled like sweat. The embrace was tight and it took me a few heartbeats to realise I was not hugging him back. My arms around his waist and my head on his shoulder I listened to his heart as it slowed down, the panic seeping out of him as my body warmed his own.

We stayed like that on the landing in the receding dark for a few moments. It was nice enough.

'Shit,' he said, pulling away. He held my shoulders lightly and looked into my eyes. For a moment I thought he was going to kiss me. 'That was terrifying. Sorry, I don't mean to be rude. But it was.'

'Yes.' I agreed, 'I'm definitely glad you were with me, Stanley.'

'Me too, Jacob.'

'*Kiss*,' a voice hissed across the way.

Chuck was standing in her bedroom door wearing only an overly large shirt which I instantly recognised as the one Uncle Harvey had been wearing in the picture I had just seen.

'He wishes,' I said flatly. Stanley offered a small snort of laughter and hit me lightly on the arm.

'What you doing?' Chuck asked, yawning.

'Going back to bed.' I told her, 'quite the adventure. I'll tell you about it later.'

'Yeah,' Stanley said, 'I'm going to go and do a couple of hours' work and then go and lay down.' He looked at Chuck from across the hall. 'Your socks are dirty.'

We all looked at her feet.

'Yeah,' she said quietly, retreating slowly into her room and closing the door.

'Goodnight, Jacob,' he said as he began his descent down the stairs. He looked worried and relieved all at once.

'You too, mate.'

Executing a tumultuous task I had sought to perform in private, I had been discovered. Fortunately I do not think any one of them suspected I was doing anything out of place for my fabricated character. We had all shared in some level of relief, though really I had not thought or felt any more than I ordinarily would and mirrored those others.

The sun was coming up by then and I relished being alone at last. My legs were sore and my brain fogged like a winter lake. In my solitude I spoke alone, quietly so to not alert any of them to what they perceived to be an oddity. In harsh yet hushed whispers did I scold myself for my carelessness.

In my experience, that hour of day where it melded so easily into the night was a blessed time for one who commits deeds such as myself. Anything strange is expected. Anything benign is strange. Anything expected is curious. And it would all be forgotten come the impending dawn.

Having silently paced and thrashed sufficiently within the confines of myself, I lay down on the hard floor and stared unblinking above. My body ached and I felt all but paralysed and yet my mind did race with its duality.

V

A storm violated the sky one evening. Ruth and I had watched it roll in over the hills one day when we had been walking Adah. The sky had begun to threaten violence and before long a curtain of thick rain had darkened the world with its approach.

As quickly as Adah's tired legs would allow, we made our way back to Crawbeth House. With such violent weather imminent there were preparations we would need to perform on the property. The windows would need to be boarded and if we had not enough food in the cupboards a trip to the village was needed and was needed urgently.

Overhead as we walked over those valleys did a bird soar. It seemed to struggle in the coming wind and at times looked as though it was painted onto that sky which had grow corpulent with mischievous clouds. For some reason I found I could hardly tear my gaze from its silhouette which fought against the wind. It was trying so desperately to go into the mouth of the destruction which came upon us then.

'What is a gull doing so far inland?' I asked Aunt Ruth. I was unsure of the specific location on the map of Crawbeth and couldn't have said where or in which direction the shore may have been.

By then, the winds had risen with a ferocity that was threatening to steal my voice away from me. Ruth's face was twisted against the barrage of wind and rain. She clutched her coat closed to her chest, the knuckles of her left hand white as ivory.

'They just come here sometimes.' She gasped as though being strangled. The answer was curt enough that I took the hint and did not say anything more.

We continued to walk, Adah's whines dashed away in the wind and over the hills just like the song of the trees or the call of the birds. Once we came to the lane which would lead us to the back of Crawbeth House. the sounds of the fledgling profane tempest became almost bearable. Again I could hear the sounds of my own ragged breaths andRuth's too.

Aunt Ruth told me that the last time there had been a particularly awful storm the roads had been shut down for weeks and she had had to wade through the lake which the road had become and walk for over an hour to reach the village.

By the time we arrived back at the house Chuck was already in the process of shuttering the windows. The ones downstairs were the most important, she told us, as it was the ground floor which was more likely to flood if the rain persisted. She had gotten a call from one of her friends in the village who had warned her of the coming calamity. Wasting no time, she had hung up and rushed to make sure all the livestock were locked away in the barn.

In the years since Harvey's death, Ruth had decreased the amount of animals they had kept on the farm for the workload had been too much, even with Stanley Pederson's assistance.

She had sold all of the cattle to Mr Pederson, Stanley's father, and had been given a fair deal. At that time the farm only boasted three pigs, four goats, two dozen chickens, and a handful of geese. Chuck had made short work of locking them away safely in the barn, but her concern for their wellbeing was apparent nonetheless.

Aunt Ruth and I fell in the door just ahead of the rain. I closed it behind me but not before taking one final look at the darkening sky. There, suspended and fluttering but lower than it had been, was the same gull I had seen. It was fighting against the wind but going no further, just staying there, caught.

We took off our coats and boots, leaving them by the door. Though it was barely midday the house was darkened under the furious clouds which had then mustered. The boards which Chuck had put over the windows only served to exasperate this change of mood.

The rain started as a few taps on the window panes at a steady pace but before a minute had passed the sound was catastrophic. There in the kitchen did the sound from the side-room's tin roof resound as though within a drum.

Initially, Adah whined in the corner but eventually seemed to relax against the rhythm of it and began snoring.

'Isn't this exciting?' Ruth declared, clapping her hands together in the kitchen, though the slap was hardly perceptible over the clamour of the brewing storm without. Ellis stood by me, tugging nervously at my shirt sleeves. I allowed myself to be a comfort to him. 'I do so love a storm. Sitting inside and listening to it beat against the house.'

'I prefer the freedom to *leave*, personally.' Chuck replied, hammering the last nail into the window frame. Beyond it the world screamed.

'Oh, don't be so grumpy, Charlotte,' Ruth laughed, 'We'll be able to spend plenty of time together, maybe play some games. I can't imagine the internet will be working so nothing but quality time for us, kids.'

Chuck groaned. Ellis growled in response. Ruth flinched at the noise as though she knew not its source.

For a moment, I even thought she looked surprised to see Ellis there, huddled next to me and hissing softly. One might think that she had not noticed him whatsoever.

With a click the lights turned off. I moved to the lightswitch, Ellis still clinging to my shirt and thus having to slowly side-step him. Flicking the switch yielded no results, as I had expected.

'Charlotte, could you try the fuses, please?' Ruth asked, rummaging around in a drawer. In the low light I could just make out her silhouette and little else. After a while, she removed a torch and turned it on. The light was a powerful and ghostly blue glow and Chuck winced as Ruth turned it directly on her face without noticing her approach.

They both yelped. Ruth laughed. Chuck did not.

'Sorry,' Ruth managed, still laughing as Chuck snatched the torch out of her mother's hand. She disappeared into the side room and I heard her arranging a ladder clumsily. 'Jacob, why don't you make some tea on the hob? I'll look for some cards.'

'It's not working!' Chuck called from the side room. She clambered down off the ladder and returned, leaving the torch upright on the table so as to cast some universal light. 'Have we got any candles?'

'I think so,' Ruth said, unsure, as she rummaged through another drawer in search of playing cards. 'Check under the stairs.'

'God, this is bullshit,' Chuck hissed as she passed me and went out into the dark hall.

The tea was poor, I had to admit. It had the taste of metal from the pan in which I had boiled the water and I had not allowed it to brew for long enough. Part of me quickly felt ashamed at my own inability to make a passable cup of tea without a kettle. I did not linger in my self-pity for long as I realised that not one of my relatives would be any more capable than I.

Whilst the rest of us played game after game of Cheat, Ellis hid under the table. The whole while he was muttering some nonsense too quietly for us to hear at all. None of us paid him much mind but on occasion I would wiggle my fingers at him and feel his sweaty little hands respond in kind or tug at one of my teasing digits.

Once I had won a fifth hand of the game in a row, Chuck put down the cards and groaned. She was bored. I felt the same and even Aunt Ruth's irksome positivity had started to show signs of wear.

'Did I ever tell you two that this place is haunted?' Ruth asked. Her face was taking on queer angles and shapes from the discarded torch.

Chuck scoffed and I rolled my eyes before nodding attentively.

'Dad?' Chuck asked, folding her arms over herself. Ruth scowled but made no further acknowledgment of her daughter's cruelty.

'When I first moved in here, after I'd married your father I started to feel it. Naturally, Crawbeth is a very old house and so it makes all sorts of noises, so I chalked it up as that initially. That was until one day when Harvey and I were working in the garden and I saw a curtain in the upstairs window flutter like someone had just been standing there, watching us.

'It was only little things at first, like a pen out of place or some of my dresses being piled up on the floor like they had been flung there in an indecisive huff. Then I started hearing people moving around at night downstairs. The first time I was so scared I couldn't hardly move. After that I got a bit braver and we would both go down and search the whole house together. We thought someone was breaking in, living in the walls. I always thought that was scarier than ghosts, some lunatic living in the house with you and coming out at night to eat your food and sit in your best chair. Not even knowing that it was happening.

'By then, I was pregnant with you, Charlotte, and everyone told me I was just having bad dreams, that it was common. The things being moved about was probably also me, they'd say, and that I just wasn't remembering what I was doing. I thought it was all bollocks of course.'

'And it was?' Chuck asked. She seemed quite genuinely enthralled with her mother's story, curiously enough for her. Ordinarily she would avoid talking to Ruth altogether or reply only in sarcastic or barbed quips but just then she stared at her mother in wide-eyed fascination.

'Well, here's the thing,' Ruth continued, clearly excited by Chuck's sudden interest, 'I was the only one convinced it was ghosts. No one believed me, especially not your father. He would just say that it was all me, that I was unwell, even after you were born. Then it all came to a head one night in November. I remember the date and time of it exactly.

'I had not yet gone to bed though Harvey had hours before. I had stayed up reading and listening to the radio. The strange happenings about the house had caused some low-level insomnia for me, anyway. Finally, at five-past-three in the morning, I decided to go to bed. That's when I heard someone walking around in the hallway. I threw open the door and yelled "AHA!"' She swung back her arm in demonstration. Ellis snarled under the table. 'She was there but not quite. This beautiful woman was sort of familiar, though I could not place her. In a way, she looked like me - or your mother,' Ruth nodded at me, 'but much older. I'm not saying she *was* either of us, that's just the comparison I made at the time. It was so odd, and I can't really describe it. I could see her there but she wasn't. It was like I was seeing her out of the corner of my eye.

'We startled each other and she backed away from me, like I was going to attack her. She disappeared suddenly after that, though, when the barking started.'

'What barking?' I asked.

'I don't know. It didn't sound like any dog I had ever heard, and I couldn't understand why there would be a dog out at that time of night. I knew Adah was upstairs with Harvey, she was just a pup back then of course. It had this horrible deep rumble in its throat and the barking sounded like it would shake the bricks out of the mortar and knock down the whole house! It was right outside the back door.

'Well, I wasn't sticking around to see whatever the hell that was. I ran upstairs and woke up your father. He grabbed the cricket bat he kept by the bed and went down to prove to me that all was fine.

'It had been raining then, just like it is now, and there were no muddy footprints as there should have been if that woman had been an intruder.' She leant back in her chair but Chuck did not relent. 'He thought I was mad, but I know what happened.'

'And did you see her again,' Chuck asked, 'the woman?'

'Nope, not ever.'

'And the dog?' I asked without even realising I had. Was it possible that it had been the same beast he encountered on the road? No, surely not. Ruth had said this all happened whilst she was pregnant with Chuck, years before my arrival at Crawbeth House. Besides, it all depended on whether or not she was even telling the truth. Stories of ghosts and phantom hounds were a morbid tradition on horrid days such as those. And regardless, Ruth was plainly not a well person, and I was unsure of for how long such had been the case. Perhaps she *had* seen these things, but whether or not it was all true or some upsetting fabrication was an entirely different matter.

Outside the rain persisted. I thought it might have even worsened as the hours had gone by. Certainly the kitchen was dark as early evening. The windows rattled and the doors creaked and moaned. From below the table Ellis responded in kind as though in conversation.

Ruth shrugged. 'I don't know,' she said, 'I never heard or saw it again after that. Through the years I've thought I've seen and heard strange things about the house and the land, but, well, I don't know... I thought it could have been... other things.' Her mood seemed to suddenly darken like a cloud filtering its wicked self before the sun. I noticed her fingers making gentle circles over her little stomach which was rounded with age and childbearing. There was such sadness in the motion that I thought it a queer thing, though did not give it much thought beyond that.

'I heard a story about it from some kids at school once.' Chuck said. 'The dog is a local legend, but apparently a bunch of folks have seen it. They said it was the dog an old farmer had. He was a rotten old bastard and trained the dog up to be just as antisocial as him. One day his wife found out he'd been *fucking* it and, naturally, she went balistic. The dog tore her to shreds. Then I think the old man died as well. So now the dog wanders the fields in the area chasing folks away.'

'Well, that's a horrid story.' Ruth said, nearly scolding her daughter. Chuck shrugged. Ellis groaned, a rattle in his throat and Ruth started somewhat at the sound of it. Chuck reached under the table and stroked his patchy hair. 'I don't know where those nasty kids get these stories but I've never once heard anything of the sort.'

'I think I saw it, you know,' I told them, 'that first night when I was on my way here. The car stopped and I thought I saw some big black dog right outside the window on the road.'

The table thumped from below.

'Right, I'm sorry I started this.' Ruth stood. 'That's quite enough. I'm not having Ellis start tearing his hair out again because of these nasty stories. Let's find something else to talk about or we can go back to Jacob beating us at cards.'

She left the room then and Chuck and I stared at each other for a moment.

'Go Fish?' she asked when neither of us had any suggestions.

The rain lasted for three days and the whole while I remained in hiding. My self-imposed exile was excruciating. The beast within me lurched forward and howled, trying desperately to be free of its chains. There was no chance of a victim at that time. Every creature worth my time was hidden away in burrows and in barns. Only the worms inched their way out of the earth to respond to the continuous thumping of the rain.

I remained hidden, a yearning pulling at my skin until it hurt. I could hardly bear it. Staying where it was dry and quiet was all I could do, trying to busy myself with menial tasks.

In that time there was little distinction between day and night and so the ordinarily nocturnal animal which was so ingrained as a part of me thrashed and whined and begged constantly.

'Patience,' I would tell it, 'after the storm comes the greenest grass. That is when the cattle graze.'

I would spend hours masturbating, trying in vain to achieve some sort of semblance of the same pleasure that I could begat from my dread art, but by the time the vile weather had passed, I was sore and exhausted and unfulfilled.

VI

I walked through the town with Aunt Ruth on market day.

Once a week, every wednesday, tradesmen and vendors would set up their stalls in the town square which was closed to traffic. The ordinarily humdrum and sleepy village would suddenly be alive with men and women yelling prices of fish and vegetables. One row of stalls was entirely populated by books organised in no particular way, the next by knock-off designer brands and cheap gold watches. There were stalls of pet toys and more still of baby clothes.

A flurry of smells coagulated and congealed there in that square. Flowers from the florists and soap made by a charming young couple who lived in a caravan on a small plot of land outside of the village. In the butcher's window did pigs hangs suspended by their rear legs and sliced in half lengthways. Below them, slabs of meat sat visceral and pink and raw before bright green plastic foliage. It was a sorry sight and one that did make me feel quite ill. There was something macabre about the way people left the shop, smiling with an already-wet plastic bag in hand and waving goodbye to the man in the striped apron. There was that morbidly curious part of myself that could not turn away from the cross section of the swine nor the legs which hung from hooks as its neighbour.

Ruth fluttered through the market in a white summer dress and floppy straw hat. She held a wicker basket over one arm and her handbag hung across her body. Her sunglasses were obnoxiously large as was the smile she wore.

She seemed a caricature of herself.

At every stall she seemed to stop to buy an apple or a fork or really anything at all that caught her eye. To everyone she spoke with an eager familiarity, asking after a family member or enquiring about their own health.

Not a one of the people she spoke to seemed to reciprocate her enthusiasm, however. It seemed that every time she turned away from a conversation, her skirts swishing and her smile broadening even more as she bid them farewell, some horrid and hushed whisper would scratch after her.

It had been nearly two weeks since Stanley and I had found Ellis on the road in the small hours of the morning and as of yet nothing had been said. Neither one of us had mentioned the incident to Ruth, it seemed, nor had we brought it up to each other. Fortunately the queer moment had done little to deter Stanley from returning to Crawbeth House on regular intervals. To my surprise, I found that I was growing quite fond of him.

We had spent several evenings sitting in the kitchen either alone or with Ruth and Chuck. I found myself becoming quite settled there with them and as I had explored the land nearby, with that part of the country as well.

The sky above was bright and wide and I felt it was doing me a lot of good being out and running errands with Aunt Ruth. It being the summer months, I had not yet been enrolled in the local school, though when it came time I was sure I would go to the very same as Chuck. As such, this meant I had had little socialisation with anyone outside of the Dunworth family but for Stanley.

To me, it was not a lonely existence, the one I had then. Social isolation was and always had been my preferred means of living. I cared very little for people my own age, believing them to be half-made and stupid, nor did I prefer the company of adults. Ordinarily, I was perfectly content with only my own quiet company, as though my very being were a magnet being repulsed from every other.

A little after midday Ruth said we should stop for tea. She had spent much of the morning prattling on and on about her cravings for cake.

'It's like when I was last pregnant,' she had told me as we drove into the village from the farm, 'all I wanted was biscuits and cake *constantly*. The doctor insisted I try to eat more balanced but I never was good at following advice. When I was carrying Ellis all I wanted was meat, but I much preferred cake.'

I chose not to question her. Ellis was her youngest son. I did not want to engage Ruth and her capricious personality around a subject that may prove to be quite sensitive, nor did I particularly want to engage. Mostly, I found, I simply did not care one way or another and just wanted her to be quiet.

We stopped in a café which I somewhat recalled from my younger days. It was a little way from the market in the village square, though I could still hear the rambunctious hubbub from it. I went immediately to find us a table whilst Ruth ordered us tea and cakes.

It was a drab little place with netting over the grimey windows and pots of misshapen sugar cubes on the table. Cloth covered each table and the chairs were of a quality one might expect to find in a nursing home. It smelled not of cake and coffee, as one might imagine, but rather of dust and despair, and a touch of mould.

Two women approaching the winter of their lives sat on a table nearby and spoke in stage whispers. They might have been much younger than they looked, but there was something about rural living which seemed to cause a drab depression about the complexion. I so infrequently found that the country air did brighten people in the way one might expect.

With them was a dog, a small westie who was staring me down with vacant and dark eyes, its whole head cocked to one side. I mimicked the tilt which appeared to spark the thing's interest in me all the more.

Besides those two and their dog, I was the only other person in the café. There was no music playing. I did not like hearing my own thoughts all too loudly.

Too easily would they flicker into screams.

'Awful woman,' One of the ladies, one wearing a light blue cardigan said, 'I had hoped she had moved away.'

'I can't imagine she ever would, Margaret. I hear her youngest has some *disorders*.' Her friend replied, whispering the last word and pursing her lips. 'She likely doesn't want to uproot him.'

'Not her youngest, mind you,' the other said, 'Gloria, you know, who lived by the park, she told me she drowned her youngest in the woods. It reminded her too much of her husband.'

'Who she *killed*.' They both made faces at each other and sipped their tea. With that, the at their feet looked up at them, sniffed the air a few times, and then returned its attention back to myself.

'Poor thing is probably better off.'

Aunt Ruth came over to me and put a tray down, passing me a tea in a stained white mug. I did not want to drink out of it.

The two old woman seemed quite uncomfortable suddenly, realising that I had heard their entire conversation, the not-so-hidden meaning of which was all too painfully apparent. Plopping a sugar cube into my drink quite nonchalantly, I smiled at them quite wryly.

'Ah! Mrs Curtis, Mrs Clarke,' Ruth smiled, not yet taking her seat but smiling at the two women. She removed her hat and her glasses and I saw then that the smile she had been wearing was not reaching her eyes. 'How are you both?'

'Oh, just fine dear,' Mrs Clarke, in the blue cardigan, told her. 'And yourself?'

'Just terrific, my nephew has come to stay with us. Well, say "hello," Jacob.'

Hardly had I been paying attention at all, so deeply invested now as I was to my staring competition with the dog whom, by the way, I was starting to assume was an aged thing. I nodded at them both and grinned in much a similar way to Ruth.

'Hello.' I obeyed.

'You remember my sister, Anne.' Ruth told them, still standing over them. The other woman, Mrs Curtis, did not look my way but stared instead into her tea, plainly too abashed to do anything but.

'*Good,*' I thought, '*bitch.*' I could not say that I was overly fond of Ruth, and there certainly seemed to be dubious rumours about her, but I knew what small villages like this were like, how rumours circulated. There was no such thing as privacy when your neighbours were the only people around for miles.

Ruth was a single mother who was also eccentric and friendless. Her husband was dead and thus tall tales would spread. I was not sure I particularly liked Ruth, but I certainly liked these strangers far less.

'Oh, of course, lovely thing, how is she?'

'Dead.' I told Mrs Clarke nonchalantly, my tether between mine own eyes and those of the dog still unbroken. She was dumbstruck at my candour. 'Ruth, your tea.' I nodded across from me and Ruth smiled at the women and took her seat.

She peeled off a bit of her cake and popped it in her mouth quite happily. She sat with her legs crossed with one rocking to a soundless beat. She sat like that, bobbing her head to a song I could not hear and tearing off chunks of cake with her fingers. Her eyes were closed and she had a faint smile on her face.

Ruth looked quite pretty like that, I supposed. Her light hair was pinned up behind her, pulling her skin taught into a younger visage. What light found its way through the dirty windows seemed to fill in any budding wrinkles on her face like filler into cracks in a wall. To me, she certainly did not look like a murderer.

We were not saying anything as we sat there then and I liked that rather a lot. Ruth seemed content in her own mind whilst I listened to the chattering old women across who then spoke in lowered voices.

'Both of them?' Mrs Clarke asked her companion, quite horrified.

'Yes. Naturally the girls are terribly upset but Carol didn't tell them what had actually happened.'

'Of course, spare them the details. So what *did* she say?'

'That they had run away. She said the fence was damaged in the storm a few weeks ago and they'd got out.'

'Poor thing. It's quite expensive to keep horses, though, so I suppose every cloud and all that. That badger might have done her a favour, you know.'

'Well, that's just it,' Mrs Curtis said, lowering her voice even more. 'We aren't sure it was an animal that did it.' Mrs Clarke gasped into her tea at that. 'There's been a whole lot of slayings like this lately, you know, and people are starting to get worried.'

'What sort of beast would do something like that?'

'I don't know, but at least it isn't happening to *people*.'

'You're right,' Mrs Clarke agreed, 'that would be awful. You're right, lucky it's only some animals. As I said, every cloud...' They both laughed.

I thought then that it was a shame my tea had cooled. I wondered how they would react if I were to throw it over them.

Ruth was on her feet. She picked up the bags which I had been carrying for her, put her sunglasses back on her face, swiped up her hat and left before I knew what was happening. I gathered the rest of our things and went out after her, unable to resist swearing under my breath at the two women as I did so.

'What was that, young man?' One of them yelped.

'I called you "cunts,"' I told them, stopping in the doorway, 'I'm not surprised you didn't hear me, you deaf old goat. Goodbye. Goodbye,' I said to each of them in turn and then to the dog: 'Goodbye.' And with that, I left, quite impressed with the steadiness of my voice.

Why I had felt so suddenly defensive of my aunt, I could not have said. I suppose that as much as I intensely disliked her more often than not, she was *mine* to intensely dislike, and not some dithering old gossips who had nothing better to talk about but for a poor woman's suffering whilst they were waiting for death.

Ruth I found outside, staring out into the street. In spite of her large sunglasses it was apparent she was crying. She did not look at me as I approached. Her bags were on the floor, much of what she had bought tumbling out. It reminded me of the foolish way my mother used to empty her handbag onto the pavement to find one thing within.

'Ruth,' I said softly as I joined her, 'what's the matter.' Standing at her side, I looked down at her things, some of which had fallen over the pavement's edge and had begun rolling into the road.

'Everything.' She hissed. 'Who's *that?*' I could not see through her glasses where she was looking but I turned across the street and swore silently. I did so largely for effect.

For a moment, as I examined the other side of the road to perhaps spy the source of Ruth's ire, I remembered again the ghost story she had told us the first night of the storm. I was still unsure if I believed what she said that she had seen, and I thought then that there may well have been a good chance that whatever Ruth had seen was indeed not there at all.

But then my doubts of my aunt's being of sound mind were dashed as I saw what Ruth plainly thought to be a most wretched sight.

Stanley Pederson was walking hand-in-hand with a pretty girl who seemed to be at an age with him. She had short dark hair and a button nose smattered with freckles. They were laughing. They looked like romance on a postcard.

'I don't know,' I lied. 'Shall we go and say "hello?"'

'No.' Ruth barked. Her teeth were clenched and her jaw was grinding on itself over and over. She turned on her heels and disappeared back up the road and into the square, leaving all the bags there.

Looking down at the mess, I decided with a groan that I should pick them up for her, if she was determined to behave quite so callow. This entire display felt all too familiar to me, though I was aware that whenever my mother would have an episode of this nature, it was ordinarily because she was already drunk.

She was making long strides through the crowd but I managed to catch up to her. My fingers hurt from where the plastic of the bags was straining against the weight of their contents and biting into my skin.

I did not manage to catch her up until I found her in the car. She was sobbing against the steering wheel. Her body was rising and falling rapidly. Her fist was beating against the dashboard. On the ground outside of the car door, her sunglasses lay shattered, one of the arms broken off entirely, as though she had stamped upon them in her rage.

'What's the matter?' I asked flatly. My patience for grieving was often limited at best and regarding a matter so minute as a love affair with a teenager gone awry I was already irked.

'It's all my fault. It's all my fault. Oh, god, I'm so sorry,' Ruth was becoming barely intelligible between sobs. I sat there silently next to her in the passenger seat. There was no point talking to anyone like this. In my experience people wanted to feel what they were feeling, at least for a little while. It was good to hurt, I was told. It was part of the experience of living, to hurt and grieve and cry and feel like you would be better off dead. If she was dead, she would not have any of that, she would lack all experience and sensation. Really, that's what most everyone feared about that final and ultimate unknown, that entire lack of self, of being as you were before you were born: nothing at all. 'Oh, god, I'm so awful. It's all my fault.'

'Is this about Stanley?' I asked her finally when she had composed herself a bit. Her face was a mess, red and puffy and wet. She looked terrible.

'What? No!' She sobbed again for a few moments and I regretted having said anything at all. This was boring. 'No, those poor horses.' I turned to her, my eyebrows raised. What the devil was she talking about? Did Ruth somehow think she was the killer? 'All of them, all the killings recently. It's all my fault!'

Since my arrival at Crawbeth House, there had been a number of killings. First had been the Pedersons' cow which Stanley's father had found butchered in their barn. Stanley had had his ideas about what had happened but we had all dismissed them as drunken paranoid ramblings. Next had been the chickens in the coop who had all been found with their heads and wings ripped away and left in a gruesome pile nearby. That had been when the suspicions had begun amongst the town as there had been no evidence of any teeth marks.

Over the last two weeks, a number of other animals had died in similar ways. One farm had lost three sheep and another had found their prized sow murdered. All had been disemboweled. Most everyone seemed to think it was a skulk of foxes and so the men and women from town had taken to shooting any they had seen immediately. Families all across the village were locking their cats inside and setting up hutches for their rabbits within their conservatories, per the police's insistence. If this epidemic was to persist, they would consider implementing a curfew.

Chuck had told us one evening that some of the kids from the village were telling stories of a feral man who lived down in the fields under the old viaduct outside of the village. Apparently he had lived there his whole life and did not even speak any language at all, so utterly wild and uneducated as he was.

'How is it your fault?' I asked, this time my interest actually peaking.

'It's my son,' she wailed, 'He's the one doing this. He's sending me a message! He's coming to get me!'

'Ellis?' I was confused. Ellis was a curious boy to say the least and Chuck had told me about the incident with the vole, but I was not convinced that he could have ever really been thought of as having committed anything quite so heinous as all that.

Over the trees of the car park emerged a number of white clouds, unspooling against the otherwise unspoilt sky.

'No, not Ellis!' She sounded almost angry at me by then. 'I had another child. He was a monster. I know it was a terrible thing to do, but, but I couldn't cope. I left him in the woods. I birthed him at home all by myself. I don't know how I survived it but I did. It wasn't human, it was a monster, more animal than anything like me. Harvey's fault, I knew, but he was dead by the time the thing was born and I couldn't do it, I couldn't...' she started sobbing again. 'I took him out to the woods and I left him there. Weeks later, when I was more myself, I realised what I had done and felt more terrible than I ever had. It was like a distant memory of the night before. The guilt ate away at me like a cancer and I could not eat any longer. I was hysterical and inconsolable, locking myself away for weeks on end, not feeding myself, not bathing, not even *seeing* the children I still had. I was going to kill myself but I couldn't orphan Chuck and Ellis. Already I was a cunt of a mother, I couldn't do *that* as well.'

Genuine surprise was not something I experienced often. Ordinarily I was expecting the worst of everyone but up until then there seemed to be a naivety about Ruth which settled my otherwise suspicious disposition. Until her sudden guilt-spurned confession I had thought her but an innocent, capricious though she was; a woman who had suffered and was making the best of a bad situation. Perhaps I could understand. She had not been in her right mind, she had acted out of desperation, a willingness to preserve her own children.

'The child died, Ruth. It's okay, the child died.' I told her.

'But what if it didn't?'

Looking back, I suppose it was then that I realised quite how mad my aunt was.

Once Ruth had calmed down we drove home in silence. It was a lovely day, one which was spoiled by Ruth's occasional sudden sobs. I thought she might swerve the car off the road and kill us both at times. Really, I did not care all that much.

My frustration with her grew to the point where I nearly hoped she would.

Ruth's abhorrent admission of infanticide had unsettled me and my opinion of her was suddenly askew. I had seen bipolar symptoms in her already dubious character, and her disgust and neglect of Ellis had become increasingly apparent in the weeks since I had lived with them, but the act which had then confessed to me made me dislike her with a sudden intensity. It was one which I did not feel I needed to force or accentuate in any way, it was a true and genuine thing that curled and snapped within my gut to the point where I could hardly turn my head to look upon her then. I remained aware of the rising and falling of her shoulders as she sobbed, sometimes silently and sometimes quite dramatically, beside me.

I wondered, on that long drive, whether or not I would actually tell Chuck of her mother's dastardly deed, though what purpose that would serve I was as of yet unsure. Instead, I elected to keep my mouth shut for the time being, and sit upon the secret, though I had made no such promise to Ruth nor did I intend to. Eventually, It may very well work in my advantage.

We had pulled into the driveway with a sudden halt and Ruth had fled into the house and immediately up to her room, slamming the door behind her. I followed her in, leaving all her bags of tat and food in the car for her to collect when she was ready. Partly, I thought, I left them there out of spite.

Chuck emerged from her painting room, the room wherein her father had died, wiping her hands clean with a dirty rag. A lovely, bassy song bloomed out from behind her. Covered in paint from her hair to her fingertips, I thought she looked quite lovely.

'What's all that?' She asked, finding me at the bottom of the stairs staring up to the landing.

'Oh, nothing.' I told her with a nonchalant shrug, 'Ruth got upset about something in town.' I did not lie.

As expected, Chuck did not question it further. By this point in her life she had become accustomed to her mother's behaviour and indeed quite visibly resentful of it. To look upon her frustrated face then one might have thought her ten years older.

Again, I considered telling Chuck what I had learned. I was certain there would be a malicious gaiety for us both, though I was not sure how Chuck would like the knowledge that her youngest sibling's death had, in fact, been her mother's doing. The resentment she felt towards Ruth's considering unloading Ellis unto the state was already visible, though perhaps not the apotheosis and origin of her disdain.

I decided to wait. Experience had taught me that it was oft better to sit upon these things, wait for their use to ferment.

My father flashed up before me, his face furious and confused at once, a cocktail I had not seen before or since. His hands were purpling from the tightness of the cuffs. The living room flashed blue and white even after the officers closed the windows so that I need not see him being taken away for his apparent misdeed.

I closed my eyes for half a heartbeat and pushed the memory from my brain. 'It was nothing, really,' I told Chuck regarding Ruth, grounding myself in my current lie, rather than the one which had gotten m

'Of course,' she muttered and went back into her room, leaving the door open. I followed her in and was instantly greeted by Adah sniffing at my hand. The dog's face was greying around the muzzle with age. Her nose was dry and her eyes milky white. Her stink filled the room more than Chuck's paint. She huffed, unimpressed with me, and wobbled over to an old dog bed which was lousy with her fur.

Even laying down seemed a labour for the old hound. She only managed a half-turn before dropping on the spot with a long and groaning exhale. I wondered, not for the first time since my arrival, just how long the old dog had left. Many people chose to put down an animal such as her once they reached a certain age, once they could no longer live their lives to their fullest, but I did not think that this would be something which would occur to the Dunworths. Most of the time, I felt that they hardly even considered her presence all that much anymore.

Chuck's "studio" was the most decorated room in the house. Each of the four walls was invisible from floor to ceiling, covered as they were by canvases of varying size. The floor was old wood which screamed and groaned from our cumbersome weight. In the center of the room was a single piece of white fabric which may have, at one time, been a sheet. An easel sat atop it with a finished piece adorning it.

Neither of the two windows had curtains.

Most every image on the walls was of one animal or another. There were cows and hedgehogs and voles and goats and snakes and plenty of Adah. It was plain enough to see the progression of Chuck's talent as she had honed her craft. She had once told me that she was trying to do at least three pieces every day over the summer holidays and the stack of blank canvases by the easel told me she had many ideas yet to birth. This had made me consider that I was perhaps only the beginning of a person, so to speak. I was not as passionate as her, nor was I as driven to any sort of creative outlet, often finding myself losing interest quickly to anything which I did not immediately find some talent in. Often I would reason that people such as Chuck were just putting on this driven front, but the results dashed that notion. Mostly I felt as though I was still being made, cooling in the clay, as it were.

On the wall to my right as I came in, across from one of the windows, was what I found the most impressive. There were dozens of paintings of Ellis. In some, those of an earlier quality, he looked pleasant and happy, a charming boy sitting pretty for a portrait. As Chuck had become more confident in her skill, the subject had become increasingly objectivist regarding her brother's personage. She used darker colours and harsher lines to portray his form. He was not looking up and smiling in those images but tilting his head to the floor and looking at her from under his angry brow. Those had more drab backdrops. Dripping blacks and reds to his back gave him that nightmarish quality which I could not escape whenever I thought of him.

I felt those more recent pieces to be a more accurate representation of him.

'Chuck,' I said, the surprise seeping into my voice without my design, 'these are very good.' She stood before her finished piece resting her chin on her fist which gripped the paintbrush.

'Cheers,' she said, not looking up. Her eyes scanned over the picture from below a furrowed brow. Her expression was not one of anger.

'Why don't you hang them around the house? Why don't you sell them?' I was actually tremendously impressed with her. I had not thought she would have such talent but the pieces were all extraordinary and boasted a particularly astute talent which one might not have expected from an adolescent.

'Why would I do that? I painted them here.' I thought she might have been gritting her teeth, but it was just her fist against her jaw as she studied the one before her. 'What do you think of this? Is it too much?'

Taking a step across the wide room I halted next to her to examine the painting which still was drying.

Like most all of her art, that one was of an animal, but I was quite shocked at it regardless. It took me a moment to realise that actually it was the fox we had found that day which had drowned by the pool. Perfectly had she depicted it, but spoiled it with the horror which hung from the corpse. Altering the reality of what we had then seen, the thing had been eviscerated, its innards hanging out of a savaged belly to become tangled around the rocks and twigs of the stream. Blood and puss and all sorts of horror evaporated into the water and became one with it. The thing's tongue hung limp out of a twisted, cracked jaw, and yet its eyes gleamed with the light of the sky reflecting off of their moistened selves.

'Gosh,' I said, 'It's extraordinary!'

'Yes,' she agreed, picking the canvas up and removing it from the easel, 'yes, I thought so too. I wonder, though, if someone might take it the wrong way.'

'What way is that?' I stood admiring the piece as she leant it against the wall, doubtless to find a place for it later.

'Maybe they'd think I'm the one doing those terrible things, I don't know. Maybe they'd think I'm admiring it. Whatever, I'm a vegetarian.' She turned around and looked at me. She stared. I did not like that. Eye contact had never been something I particularly excelled at but I forced myself anyway. After a few long seconds I found the whole thing rather painful and had to break the gaze.

'What?'

'Can I paint you?'

'Maybe one day. I'm not feeling up to it right now.'

Chuck shrugged.

'Whatever.'

Aunt Ruth did not come out of her room that evening, nor would she for several days.

I took it upon myself to cook for the others. Chuck continued painting in her room for several hours before coming to join me in the kitchen. She told me she just wanted to be there with me for company, a sentiment which I supposed was agreeable enough.

Ellis' presence was fittingly sparse until I called him for dinner. Where he had been I could not have said but really it made no difference to me. Little did I know of how Ellis filled his time and, much like his sister and mother, I suppose I did not pay anything he did much heed.

The thought of Ruth's abandoned child did not pass from my mind. Of course, I was all too aware that it was not causing those wretched deaths, not all those years after having been left to die of exposure. It was certainly an interesting notion, some wretched poroniec prowling the countryside. The very image that such an idea conjured seemed albut unholy and a foul thing indeed.

My mind's eye did paint a foul image of the scene over and over in my mind, and I found the babe to be interchangeable in that with the fox of Chuck's painting. On some level, I knew I should have felt something more like sympathy for Ruth. She plainly was not a well person. No happy, healthy person would do something quite so hellish.

Sitting with my cousins that evening was nearly pleasant. Chuck and I spoke uninterrupted through the duration of the meal and beyond. We even seemed nearly attentive to one another. It was the difference of not having Ruth's constant repetitive babbling. Even the nature of the conversation was different. Chuck seemed to avoid the dreary topics she so often favoured and instead we discussed literature, memories from our childhoods, and once we had eaten, Chuck chose some music for us to play.

Very little noise came from upstairs. Ordinarily when Aunt Ruth entered into what we had taken to calling her 'episodes,' the racket and comotion she caused behind that closed door was more unbearable than the disquieting mood which settled over the whole house. She was disturbingly still that evening and thus she would remain for several days yet. Part of me wondered if she had taken her own life, so wracked by guilt and shame as she had been, or perhaps fear that I would go to the authorities with her ghastly secret. I did not deign to share my concerns with Chuck, nor did I venture upwards to look in upon her and check on her wellbeing. Whatever response she would give me would be wholly negative and in no way constructive, I knew.

That time of Aunt Ruth's confinement passed without complaint. The three of us ate at least two meals together each day and beyond that busied ourselves with singular entertainments. Chuck continued to paint and by then, in our reformed enjoyment of our kinship, she had taken to calling me to inspect each one as it was completed. I had a philistine's eye when it came to art but it seemed to me that actual critiques were not what she sought, rather Chuck desired praise. With an all but absent mother and a deceased father, it was understable. Plainly, she had had none for a long while. I sincerely doubted that Ruth would ever show much of an interest in her daughter's budding talent, and in all likelihood Chuck had long since halted her attempts at gaining her mother's support.

Ellis seemed most content in the garden during the day though I made sure to summon him in for supper and to not allow him out into the dark again. I also ensured doors were locked every night, a thing which surprised Chuck simply because he mother had never seemingly done so. The solitude of Crawbeth House had apparently been all the security that they had ever needed from what dangers the outside world might harbour.

I did not feel it prudent to explain that I did not have concerns for what was without, but rather what darkness was there, under our very roof.

He did not require as much care as I had initially assumed and offered little in the way of protest when either Chuck or myself told him to bathe. He would sit in the bath in a nearly catatonic state, staring through the water to his bare legs which mutated under the shifting surface. One of us would be with him as he sat there, half submerged in the water. We would wash his hair as often as possible, though made sure to treat his scalp tenderly for his violent mistreatment of it had surely made the skin tender at least and mutilated at worst.

Perhaps there was even a sense of reward for caring for those two as I did in the days of Ruth's self-imposed exile. I felt the weight of something leave me, though what it was I could not have then said. It was a pleasant feeling in a particular peculiar way, like laying on a cold floor after a most hideous bout of vomiting.

Stanley helped on the farm during a few of those days, but without Ruth to direct him his work was general and he found himself finishing earlier and earlier each day. He and I would drink together in the kitchen or lay on the grass in the garden together whilst Chuck painted us and Ellis watched the insects buzz about him.

Those were the most pleasant of afternoons, feeling our skin baking lightly under a film of sweat brought on by the growing summer sun and enjoying one another's presence whilst remaining wholly separate entities.

One particularly jolly day the four of us walked through the fields and though we headed in the right direction, Chuck did not take us to the pool, nor did she even mention it. I chose to not bring it up and leave it as her own sanctuary.

Ellis even seemed to become more responsive to us. No longer did he lack communication entirely, but soon his growls and grunts became nearly intelligible and through their primal and guttural non-words did we begin to discern some sort of meaning and indication as to his wants and needs. Perhaps this sudden ability to in some way communicate was our own devising, or perhaps some sort of mental barrier had been broken by our joyous days and care of our less fortunate peer.

Without Ruth's interference, Ellis seemed more a member of the family and less some dread shadow hanging over Crawbeth House. That underlying fear of him, I knew, had hitherto been fostered entirely by his mother, It was a chaotic energy we had then ourselves syphoned.

I think that perhaps those were the loveliest days I had had since my arrival at Crawbeth and my reintroduction to the Dunworths.

All that time we heard not from Ruth. I was not even sure he had left her room for a glass of water. Chuck had taken to leaving meals outside her bedroom door and announcing their delivery but come morning one of us would take them away again and give them to Adah, having been entirely untouched by Aunt Ruth.

'Should we go in there?' Stanley asked me one evening. He had come over for dinner with us and had stayed there talking with me long after Chuck had retired for the evening. We both sat on the green sofa, our legs outstretched and besides each other's. He had brought whiskey as was his want and after a few hours my cousin had begun to fall asleep. I had put her to bed and left a glass of water by her for I knew she would sorely need it come the morning.

'Chuck says no.' I lied. Still the thought of the abandoned baby rattled me. The initial shock of Ruth's vile confession had ebbed and I thought less and less of it, but there was a righteous part of me which did feel that her self-imposed exile was punishment, though I had not felt that such was nearly fitting enough for her sickening crimes.

Naturally, I still had not mentioned this nightmare to any of the others, which I suppose made me her judge and jury all at once.

'Yeah, right, probably for the best.' He touched the rim of his glass nervously, pinging his finger against it as he thought. I liked that about Stanley, it was plain enough to everyone around him when he was thinking. I had seen him before trying to read. His brow furrowed and he mouthed words as though he simply could not keep them inside, like a child reading a book. I found that quite endearing. 'I feel like I haven't seen her in a while now.'

'You know she was just here, right?' I joked. He rolled his eyes and kicked me softly.

'You're never that serious, are you?' He said, sipping his drink again.

It was not something I had ever before been accused of. My mother had always detested my sarcasm for she found it just another aspect of my animosity towards her. In school I had not had an abundance of friends for so many of my peers had found me to be overly grave. Never had I minded as much, finding the solace I craved from my own company. My sombre demeanor had hardly been agreeable to other children and my teachers had thought me odd, though were proud of my success as a result of my spiritual isolation.

Really, I did not agree with Stanley's observation. I was a terribly serious young man. Only then did it strike me quite how little he knew of me.

'Nah,' I shrugged.

'I think I'm going to end it with Ruth.' Stanley told me, lowering his voice so she could hear him not. I thought the caution needless as my aunt was far on the other side of Crawbeth, behind closed doors and her own self loathing. He put his glass down on the floor and sat up a bit. I did the same. I did so because he did.

'Right now? I don't think...'

'No, you dickhead, not *right now*. I've just come to realise lately that we want different things. I've been thinking about it since that night you and I found each other on the road. I like her, sure, she's a good lady, when she isn't being a loon, but that isn't enough.'

'I see,' I wasn't really paying attention. I was quite drunk and just the movement of his face as he spoke I found quite mesmerising. It was hardly the first time I thought Stanley to be more attractive than he was interesting and it could have hardly been much of a secret how immensely bored I was of the subject of Ruth Ellen Dunworth

'I don't know, man. There's things I want to do, and I think she just wants someone to help her, really. Hell, maybe she wants me to replace Mr Dunworth. But I still think of myself as a teenager, you know?'

'I suppose no one really takes you all that seriously when you're eighteen.' I agreed, 'You're an adult, but barely and certainly not to those older than you, and you're not a child anymore.'

He smiled softly at me.

'Well, that's exactly right.' He agreed. 'And I think of Chuck and Ellis as my friends more than my potential *children,* you know?' He paused then and looked at me. Again, I did not well like the extended eye contact, but Stanley was handsome enough that I did not entirely mind it for a few moments. 'You're pretty wise for your age, Jacob.' He concluded.

'I've had to be.'

'Yeah, right.'

We did not say anything for a few moments after that but instead just looked at eachother. It was odd. He seemed content but after a few moments the intensity of his soft and searching gaze was too much and I swung my legs over the side of the sofa. His gaze, I thought, was developing that glassy quality that does tend to come over those of drunks. I remembered my mother's eyes, particularly as her life ebbed away across the bathroom floor.

'I'm going to piss.' I said, stumbling out of the room.

I was gone for a short while. Suddenly, I found myself losing my composure. That lesser part of myself, that uninhibited and all too human emotional side of myself, it was something which revolted me. I had to right myself, maybe even step outside for a few moments, breathe the night air and bathe in the bright burning brilliance of the Mil ky Way.

When eventually I returned to the living room, walking down the hallway towards the door, I heard panicked voices from therein.

'I don't fucking know! Go outside! I'll call someone, *go!'* It was Chuck.

Stepping back into the room I found them both pulling on their coats with a clumsy and desperate severity. Stanley was confused, his eyelids heavy from drink and yet he was suddenly more alert. Chuck looked terrible. She had barely dressed before coming downstairs from her room and her hair was all in disarray. I asked them what was happening.

'The fucking barn is on fire!' Chuck barked before shoving past me, out the back door and into the glowing night.

The agonized screams of those within had already started to shatter the nighttime peace. The three of us ran from the house into the cool night air to blankety ourselves in that most violent song.

It had taken moments to start the inferno. It's eagerness to burn had startled me, though after a moment I sank into the warm joy of the universe accepting my godly act. For to take a life, and so many at once, surely that was a way of playing God?

I had dreamt of it, feeling my fate entwined with that place. Stars eons old knew I would be there to set that spark and consume the viciousness of that hungry blaze. It was wondrous and divine, to have those dead and burning eyes flicker and twinkle at my beautiful performance, this picturesque piece I did then create. Soon, as the smoke became one with the night, they shut themselves to it and shied away into the ether from whence they had so suddenly appeared.

Until the moment I had done it, even I knew not that I would do so but the fleeting glimpse I got of those hungry glowing tongues lapping at the old wooden barn I knew it to be destiny. There was an eroticism about it, the way the fire lapped at the skin of the barn and tore away its painted visage. I had to turn away from it before the others found me there, love in my eyes and my genitals quickening.

As per their nature, the inhabitants came to stare helpless as they watched my finest work. They knew not it was me who did then rend apart their lives. If it had not drawn them to me I would have howled with laughter like the hyena. I held myself from the cold in a heated autophilic adoring embrass. Oh, there was a love I felt I had never known and it warmed me even more than the flames had.

My dreams paled in the ecstasy of the moment. Bloody bright locks sealed the half-sentient lives within that place to a most terrible doom and I was glad of it. Their screams from behind the cracking wood were smothered by the roaring of the old barn as it fell apart around itself. It all sang in the night in a most nightmarish melody and I wept to the music of it, my whole body shuddering.

My face was warmed by it and I tasted the salty tears on my own cheek as I revelled.

VII

Certainly I felt that in my waxing years I had too early an introduction to violence. When others my age, still perceiving the world purely as an unintelligible blur of shapes and colours, were being loved and held to a comforting breast, I was witness to the nightmarish assaults my family were performatively inflicting upon one another. It would be a few years until that horror would reach me, but still too early did I know of it.

As such, the ghastly sights, sounds, and stenches which were erupting from the cataclysm did not quake me. That was even though I probably should have felt something like sentiment. The barn had been erected by Uncle Harvey's own father to whom Crawbeth House had once belonged. A recollection of a photograph came to me then, as my actual vision was blinded by tears begat by the harsh smoke. Harvey, his father, and my own father were standing side by side along the roof of the barn, tool belts about their waists. They were shirtless and smiling broadly.

It must have taken them weeks, months perhaps, to build the thing. One spark was all it had taken to undo all of that.

Standing before something as shattering as that blaze I felt as a small child. I'm sure the others felt the same, though if such were the case then we were all too aghast to utter as much. There was nothing any of us could do to prevent it, we just had to watch it happen. By the time we had gathered outside the barn had been entirely ablaze and there was no hope of saving those trapped within. They were all to burn.

Each of us was intent to watch the barn burn, despite how inadvisable as we knew the notion to be.

Chuck had gone back into the house to call for help but due to Crawbeth's remote location and the village's lack of municipal services, no one would be there before the hour. They told us to get as far from the barn as we could and do not attempt to put it out. I had tried to usher Stanley and Chuck inside, intending to get Ellis and Ruth and bring them to the back garden in case the blaze were to spread, but Stanley had been almost inconsolable. He thought only of the death which then polluted the air with its stink and ghoulish melody.

He stood firm as though planted there into the ground telling me he wanted to make sure the fire did not spread over to the main house. By then the roof was collapsing under the destructive and hungry calamity, roaring as it did so. Try as I might, my convincing him that he could do little to prevent the spread were it to happen yielded few results and he stood sure and shocked and afraid.

By when the fire brigade arrived the barn was all but gone, though the fire raged still, fed as it was by the corpses within the barn and the hay upon which they had once fed. They wasted no time getting to work extinguishing it, pushing us back so that they could douse the flames. Stanley, Chuck, and I had stood there watching it happen, helpless and mesmerised by it. Ellis had been left in his room once Chuck was sure that he was undisturbed by what was happening outside.

Ruth had still yet to make an appearance. Once I thought I saw the curtain jostle as though someone within were observing us, but when I focused on the room within, beyond the fiery glare of the window, I saw no one at all. I thought presently of the spectre which had at one time accosted Ruth herself, and wondered. Surely I had not seen any phantom or ghoul, but a fearful and ashamed woman, lost in the grasping tentacles of her own guilt.

Later, when it was all done, we three sat inside with a number of the firefighters. I had made everyone tea and the sound of it being drunk was almost deafening over the crushing silence. We were all aware of the loss of life which had just occurred, but it seemed as though everyone was too uncomfortable to say anything about it.

The whole house stank of smoke and indeed I saw it had gathered on the windows, marring the vision of the dark early morning hues. The police would be joining us soon to inspect the smouldering remains though the fire brigade had found little to give any evidence of what may have begun the blaze. This, we had all agreed, seemed more suspicious than if they had.

By then the sun was emerging from its nightly grave and the kitchen was beginning to fill with a dull blue light. Stanley and Chuck sat in silence for the most part, Stanley barely touching his tea but instead examining its stillness in his hands. It was odd to see him thus and I might have thought it uncomfortable for its alienness were I not presently so consumed with my own thoughts.

'You guys don't need to wait up, you know,' one of the men said, 'it's been a long night. If you want to go and get some sleep we can come and wake you when the officers get here.' He was a kindly looking man, large in frame and with big rosey cheeks. I did not know if the colour was an effect of the blaze or the perpetual chill which so often engulfed Crawbeth. I would have thought one of us would have objected but almost immediately Chuck rose out of her seat. It scraped along the floor with a grinding violence. Most everyone in the room winced at the screaming sound. I then stood too and put my hand on Stanley's arm, nodding at him. He had not been listening.

'Thank you all,' I said because the others had already left the room. I could hear them both slowly going up the stairs with a steady simple rhythm. 'Please help yourselves to whatever you'd like. I doubt we will sleep but, thank you.'

Some of them told me how well I had done, how brave I had been. I thanked them again and left, eager to lay down.

It was only then, on my way upstairs, that I remembered the amount we had drank earlier on. My head had started to hurt by that point, but I hadn't the energy to return to the kitchen for a glass of water. Instead I would just bear the pain for the next few sleepless hours.

On the landing, Stanley was saying goodnight to Chuck. He hugged her silently and she gripped onto his strong arms, afraid. I joined them because I thought it the right thing to do. We all stayed there like that for a little while before Chuck pulled away. She breathed deeply and closed the door of her room behind her.

After checking in on Ellis and deciding that he was just fine within, I went into my room and Stanley hovered there on the landing. He had plainly been about to try Ruth's door but had thought better of it.

'Come in,' I told him, leaving the door open behind me. He did and shut the door behind him.

From the window I watched the world. The lights of the vehicles outside brought the room alive again and again and again with bright blue electric flares. There were two engines parked there below my window. I thought it impressive they had managed to fit side-by-side in the drive, wide as it was. By now the sky was turning a pale and yet muted colour. It was a new day. Stanley sat on the edge of the bed.

'Thank you, Stanley.' I said, 'thank you for your help this evening. I appreciate it very much, and I mean that.'

'I didn't do anything.' He said, his voice shaking. I did not look at him for fear that he might be crying. I never dealt particularly well with the emotions of other people. It seemed to bring out a rage in me which I could not cope with and so thought it only prudent to excuse myself until the flurry was over. 'There was nothing I could do. Oh, god, all those animals…' I looked at him then and my stomach turned at such a pitiful sight. Tight whitening fingers gripped his head, running through his hair and pulling at his skull. His back rose and fell with each shuddering breath. While he was not looking I mimicked this useless way of breathing to see if I could do it as well as he. My form in the mirror seemed convincing enough though only could I see a curious flashing silhouette formed against the flashing lights. It looked as some ghastly ghoul, looming over Stanley's melancholy self and mimicking each movement with an insensitive mockery.

Kneeling down before him I gripped his wrists and pulled his hands away from himself to hold them in my own. He did not want to look up at me. I was okay with that. I was not so sure I wanted to look at anyone, anyway.

'There was nothing you could have done. Don't be silly. There's nothing any of us could have done but what we did. I know it's terrible, but it's done.' My voice was low, each word precise. It did not sound like me, I felt as though I was playing a part, but I was playing it tremendously well.

He looked up at me, puzzled. His eyes were wet and his lips were trembling and puffy. Was he terrified of me? Many times in my life had I seen that exact look on someone's face, yet still I could not quite gauge it. No, surely not. He had no reason to be. That look though, it was simply too akin to others I had seen in various circumstances.

For several heartbeats he did not say anything. Nor did I. We just stayed like that, our faces a few inches from one another, his distraught and twisted and moist, and mine motionless as a marble statue.

I kissed him.

He pulled away at first and looked at me again. His eyes were wide and then flickered over my face. There was a visible unsureness and a flash of anger which relaxed as quickly as it had come.

He kissed me.

Salty and slick with his tears, it was not how I had pictured that moment in my erstwhile fantastical planning of it. It was not overly pleasant at first but he pulled me closer to him as we stood and suddenly it was.

My fingers grabbed onto his shirt. My nails tore through to his skin. I felt him wince. His tears slathered my own face but I couldn't help but smile at the irony of it. Ruth was in the next room, catatonic and entombing herself in a sepulcher of superstitious guilt. Through one wall there I was, being undressed by her lover.

I could not help myself but to laugh at the wickedness of it.

With a most violent start I awoke as Stanley was pulled naked from my bed by his ankle.

Before my eyes adjusted I thought it was Death for the assailant's form was emaciated and white as bone. A dressing gown hung loose over a bony form, ribs protruding and a sunken stomach. It trailed behind her like the wisps of a shredded cloak, exposing her unkempt sex and freely exposing the stink of her.

Ruth had emerged from her room after beyond a week's absence.

She clawed and punched at Stanley. He blocked her attacks with his forearms which were already darkening from my own passionate touch. She crouched over him screaming in what was one terrible fetid breath. Again and again and again her bare foot connected to his ribs. I could hear the air being knocked out of him. All sorts of terrible things came from her mouth as she tried to drag her dirty nails across his face.

Like a pale cowl her hair fell down over her but even through that cascade could I see the rabid madness within her. If she was a dog she would have been shot. Her eyes were wide and her yellowing teeth bit into her upper jaw.

Stanley yelled for her to get off him, that he could explain, that he was sorry. Still she berated him with a cantankerous poem of foulness. He sobbed and heaved and wailed and begged her all at once.

I watched from the bed, my nakedness not covered at all by the sheets those two were becoming tangled in. He was bleeding by then from his mouth, from his arms, from his chest.

My foot connected to the side of her head and she fell away from him, taking down the bedside table which she had grabbed for. Ruth hit into the wall with a thud which shook the house and Stanley scrambled to the dresser on the far side of the room to be away from her, unable to stand as he pulled himself along in his desperate fleeing like some terrified and rabid animal. He stood there by the window, gasping and sobbing, his body tense and paralysed.

Ruth pushed herself back up, growling like her son might. She reached a sinewy arm for the lamp which had fallen as she had. I beat her to it.

Her hands, though thin, possessed a manic strength as they seized my ankle. I did not move as she pulled at me, rooted to the floor like a most ancient tree.

Teeth sank into my shin. Blood gushed instantly. I felt her pulling away the skin without opening her jaw.

I made no sound of pain, even as I watched her do so.

The lamp broke over the back of her head.

Ruth was taken away by the police fairly promptly after that.

As a minor I knew my actions would not have repercussions for me. Besides, I had a witness to say that all had been done in self defence. For many years I had been aware of this fact. Once we become adults, our ability to fight and defend ourselves is hindered by the confines of the law. To me, it seemed, it was one of our basest instincts, to defend ourselves even with violence.

My mother had once told me that I should get all my aggression out before I came of age. I should fight regularly, give in to that primal and brilliant violent desire, otherwise I would be wasting my childhood.

Very little of what she had said had I ever paid much heed to, but that once became one of my most wanton of vices.

Once I had grown old enough, I had stood up to her own terrible ways and had taken to answering in kind to them. I had done so again and again until she had died. The sound of her head bouncing off the basin would always unsettle any moment of peace I could find, as would the wetness of her warm blood seeping between my toes over the bathroom floor.

Chuck had flown into the room after I had hit Ruth a second time. With the force between the blows I was surprised that I had not killed her.

At the sight of her mother incapacitated, Chuck did not react how one might expect a child to. She nodded to me, then removed herself calmly from the room to fetch the men in the kitchen who, by then, were already on the landing. They pushed past her and found us there.

My ankle was bleeding quite badly by then. My blood was smeared across Ruth's face and her hands were red with Stanley's own fluids.

Stanley.

Poor Stanley.

He was taken away by one of the fire fighters. He was hysterical, sobbing and wailing and clearly in some state of shock. One of the others snatched up the sheets and took them out to him to wrap him up. Myself, however, I remained unphased by my nudity though everyone else in the room seemed suddenly quite abashed by it.

I would not feel the deep cuts left in my palm by the broken lamp I still held for several hours.

My back rose and fell with each shuddering breath.

Just as Stanley's had as he had sat on my bed mourning the loss of the barn's contents a few hours before.

Just as Ruth's had when she had told me about abandoning her child in the woods to die.

There was no anger there within my own self, no malice or sadness or shock. This was exactly what I thought would happen. Simply I was surprised at how precisely the whole scene had played out, mirroring my expectations entirely.

That calm remained with me as I was escorted out of the room by another one of the men. Yet another followed and draped a dressing gown about me.

They told me to sit down right there at the top of the stairs. I told them I wanted a cigarette. One of them, I do not know which one, gave me one of his own. I smoked it right there on the stairs and was surprised they did not protest sheerly out of irony. I think the brutality of the incident had granted unto me some leniency.

Chuck dealt with things from there.

I had been in the garden for several hours laying flat on my back with my arms at my side as though I was being measured for a coffin. I watched the clouds shift together and unravel overhead. I listened to the song of the trees and the silence of the country, wondering how far away those soft slow colossi actually were. Without the clamour from within the barn which had hitherto disturbed that serenity it was quite lovely to lay there, all but unliving.

A fetid stink had tumefied the air but I relished in that morose odour.

'Stanley's going to stay with us for a few days.' Chuck's voice said. I did not look up or around to see her approach but rather watched heaven roll on by past my eyes. 'The police wanted us to go to Pederson's place but I told them it wasn't a good idea to put that much strain on Ellis. Fuck knows how he's going to take all this.'

'*He won't even notice.*' I thought but said nothing because I shouldn't.

'He's going to go and get some of his things and will be back this evening.' She was sitting next to me then. I still did not look to her.

It was the done thing to ask how she was. I did not.

The world was silent. It was lovely.

'I did not know,' Chuck said slowly, 'about you and Stanley.'

'There is no *me and Stanley.*' I said, mimicking her. 'I just wanted to see if I could.'

'Oh,' She said. I felt her lie down beside me.

We did not say anything else.

My finest work so far. There was nothing there anymore, the air was empty of the chaotic orchestra of life. It was delicious. Inhaling deep of the smoky air I could almost taste them, their pain and their tears, that final nightmare moment of their lives.

It was delicious.

Everything in the house had imploded with hysteria more so even than I could anticipate. I knew the fire would change things in a rapid and sadistically brutal transition but I had not anticipated to what degree.

They had turned on each other as though they had until then been waiting for an excuse. The woman had been taken away by the authorities in a rage I had not thought her capable of in the time I had been watching them. She had a wild look about her bulging and bloodshot eyes. Her teeth were gritted and bared through peeled-back lips. With a powerful will of murderous vengeance she had struggled though her hands were cuffed behind her back. I thought she might break her own arm. I hoped she would, just so that I could have seen it happen and hear the sudden agony of it.

Like birds they all flocked together then for safety. Even by then I had not decided my next move until it delivered itself to me quite willingly.

I had again been standing amidst my work, the blackened wood and the grey ash breaking so lightly and effortlessly under my bare feet. I knew that under all that incinerated debris were dozens of extinguished lives.

The old bitch waddled up to me on unsure legs and sniffed the air around me. It felt like an unfair advantage, her lack of sight. Regardless, I could not deny such a willing sacrifice.

From that beautiful smoldering carnage, I led her away into the night. I could perform my work in private. Her trust of me did make it all the less challenging.

She struggled along with me as we walked. I knew what I did would be a release for her.

VII

'Ellis is gone!' Chuck cried, falling into the kitchen.

I had asked her to fetch him as I stood over the hob preparing him a breakfast of sausages and bacon and nothing more. Stanley sat at the kitchen table in pajamas. He had a cup of tea before him which he was not drinking, glaring at it motionless as he had in the small hours of the morning the barn had burnt.

The day before the three of us had worked together to clear some of the charred debris which had once been that wooden structure beyond the house. Clearing the corpses had been an unpleasant job but we had made short work of the burial by scattering the bodies in groups in large graves across one of the nearer fields. In a few months time, the bodies would break down and feel the soil and the fields would become a brighter green than ever.

As we had done so, Ellis had watched us from the driveway.

'What?' Stanley asked. I truly believed he had not heard her.

Stanley had been preoccupied over the last few days talking to the police. They had asked him to give a statement regarding Ruth's assault on him but after an evening alone with his thoughts he had decided not to. The repercussions did not seem worth it to him. What would become of the rest of us if Aunt Ruth was taken away from us?

'He's gone!' She yelled again, stepping in and out of the kitchen like an excited dog, demanding that we follow. 'I went to get him, like you said, and he's not there!'

I shrugged and rolled a sausage over. The oil spat at me and I snatched my hand away, hissing back at it between clenched teeth.

'Oh, you know what he's like,' I said, nonchalant, 'he's gone wandering around the garden. Have you tried there?'

'Of course I have, you idiot.' She barked back at me. 'He knows not to go far from the house without one of us. Oh, god, oh, *fuck*.' Chuck's panic was tedious. I rolled my eyes and followed the kitchen around to the side room. He was not in there.

'Stanley, would you please go and check Aunt Ruth's room and the rest of the house, every nook and cranny? I'll check the western field and Chuck, you continue to panic because that's *tremendously* helpful.'

She threw a slipper at me as I left through the front door.

I had assigned Stanley the simpler of the tasks for I had seen in the few day's since Ruth's assault on him that his capacity had lessened. He needed simple instructions now, spoken plainly and often repeated. Certainly I found it curious to see him so lost in thoughts as it was not fitting with his person. His days seemed consumed now with an inner turmoil and regret. Every day, sometimes hourly, I could see him going back and forth over and over about his decision to not press charges.

I had found the conversation, the repetition of it, overly irksome.

He had come to my bed for comfort from then on, but after the first night, I no longer found myself desiring him intimately. His sudden lack of any personality I had found dull and repetitive, though not so utterly infuriating as his constant crying.

I do not think it cruel to say that a pathetic person is not an attractive one.

Occasionally he would try to kiss me in the night and I would let him but make no move to reciprocate. He would put his arms around me and lay there, quietly crying. The wet would sit on my chest and rest within my clavicle. It would congeal there to a mournful putrid puddle.

Not once did I ask him about it. I did not care for it and, had I been more cruel, I might have told him to sleep elsewhere, perhaps Ruth or Ellis' room. They clearly were in no need of their space.

Despite my skepticism, it quickly became apparent that Chuck's fear was not unfounded. Ellis was nowhere on the property. We searched the whole house, turning out cupboards and wardrobes, knowing of his proclivity to hide in dark places like a wounded cat. Chuck climbed into the loft despite my insistence that there was no way he could have closed the hatch behind him given its design.

Stanley checked the eastern and southern fields whilst I walked the long path back to the main road, thinking the whole time of the great black dog which had come so close to my window that first evening. I had not forgotten about the thing, that terror which even the driver did not seem to notice. Since my arrival at Crawbeth House, I had not heard the howls of a wild hound, as Chuck had once insisted she had herself. As the weeks had gone by I had begun to think that perhaps the thing had actually been no more than a nightmare. I *had* been incredibly tired during that long drive from the train station and I knew that in fact I had fallen asleep several times in its duration.

I got to the road where it forked, one direction heading into the village and the other further into the unpopulated countryside. I knew there was little I could do to help beyond there. We would need a car. We would need several cars and search parties. I was not sure how fast he was and we did not know how long he had been travelling. By now he would be truly lost.

We spent the rest of the day searching. Once we were satisfied that Ellis was not in the immediate area we gathered back at Crawbeth and decided on our next move.

Chuck called the police but the connection had been unclear. She screamed down the phone about the situation and hung up, furious. We did not know if anyone was coming.

Stanley, not wanting to waste any more time, decided to return to his own house and tell his father to go to the village and get some help.

Chuck was reluctant. She did not want all those people around the house. Everything was a disaster, she said. The barn was now but a scorch on the ground and Ruth was gone.

In the end, her brother's wellbeing had outweighed the need for privacy and she had consented. Stanley had wasted no time and fled back to his parent's house.

'I would not feel any better if she was here.' Chuck said. Her forehead was pressed against the table. She was agitated and yet felt powerless and without direction. By then she must have been exhausted. My attempts at feeding her had been fruitless though it was clear she needed the energy. 'She's always been an awful, useless cow since Dad died. I've cared for Ellis through all of my teens whilst she's floated about with an empty head or locked herself away in a melodramatic waking coma. And it doesn't help, her obvious terror of her own son. If it wasn't for Stanley nothing would get done around here. I hate her. *I hate her.*'

Nodding was all I could offer just then as she looked up to see it whilst the conversation lulled.

She searched my face which I had made into a mask of pity just in time. It was one I had become so accustomed to seeing upon my peers over the last few years that I felt I could replicate it perfectly. The mechanics of my face emulated what empathy was and it worked. Chuck covered her mouth and shook her head. 'I'm so sorry, Jacob,' she said then. Her voice did not break, even when she was ready to cry. That's what I liked about Chuck, she so rarely allowed for her emotions to better her. Likely having grown weary of her mother's own. 'I'm being so terribly ungrateful.'

'Let me tell you something,' I said, as though to a child, 'I hated my mother too. My father wasn't much better either, as you well know.' Chuck smiled at that and I could not help but smile too. I thought she would like it if I did. 'You should get some sleep, Chuck.' I told her.

The lie had come easy. To form a bond with Chuck, remind her of the story I had spun, it certainly shut her up a bit.

For a moment the thought of protest danced across her eyes but only for a moment. She nodded and pushed herself up on unsure legs. At that moment I thought she looked thirty years older.

'Thank you, Jacob.' She said before she left, 'I dread to think how different things would be without you here with me.'

I returned her smile and nodded.

Night had gathered and I sat in the darkness. Stanley had not returned with the posse he had promised. The house certainly seemed bigger without the mere fact of the others' existence within. I had sat in the chair in the living room looking out the window to the garden for hours, curiously serene, given the situation.

My musings had been quite sour in their nature. Ellis' disappearance was stirring all sorts of memories within my mind. Particularly, I found, I thought of my father. I relived sitting there in my room as I told the officers my story. Through the crack in the door I could see him being taken away. His head was hung low then. He had looked to me only ever so briefly with a piercing twist of hate. Surely he had known that there was nothing more he could possibly do.

After all, it had been my word against his.

It was quarter-past nine when three sharp knocks came upon the front door, wrenching me back to the present. I had not noticed myself sitting in the dark though I must have been for several hours by then. So utter was that blackness that I could not even see my own hand before my eyes.

Walking through the house I did not turn any of the lights on until I came to the kitchen. Beyond the window I could see a police car. *'Good,'* I thought. Though the hour was late we could at last begin a true search for Ellis. The three of us scrambling about in fields and forests would serve no one.

I opened the door to two officers standing with Aunt Ruth between them. She did not look herself, nor did she appear as the ghoul which had assaulted Stanley in my bedroom just three nights previously. Really, I should have felt furious that she was there, or perhaps afraid of her or her wrath upon discovering that we had lost her surviving son.

I felt none of those things.

Ruth stood between the officers in a light grey jumper and equally bland trousers. She wore simple fabric trainers and her hair was tied away from her face which seemed to have aged several years. Everything about her looked grey, her eyes in particular. Of course, it was probable at least that she had not had much decent sleep.

Only once, as I opened the front door, did she look up and beyond that she studied the ground. Somehow, despite the state of her, there was an air of youth about her I had only seen thus far in forced quantities.

Stepping aside, I allowed the three of them to enter. Ruth went immediately to the kitchen and poured herself a glass of water. She drank it down before sitting herself at the table and saying nothing. I watched her do so from the hallway where I spoke with the officers.

They told me that as neither myself nor Stanley wished to proceed with any sort of prosecution that they had no grounds to hold her any longer. She had been referred to a councillor in the town an hour away who she would begin by seeing twice a week. It had been plain enough, they told me, that she was suffering from a state of chronic grief. That, combined with her already challenging personality disorders was causing her mental state. They would perform regular checks either by telephone or in person and these would be at random, unscheduled intervals.

Before long they had left and I returned to the kitchen. I had not mentioned Ellis, reasoning that I was too frantic and exhausted to think upon multiple matters at once, as they had begun to unfold so rapidly. Aunt Ruth and I both stared at each other and I did not know then if we were about to fight or hug.

'I'm sorry, Jacob,' she said almost too quietly for me to hear.

'So am I, Ruth,' I lied. I felt nothing about what had happened, but it seemed the right thing to say. From my mother's beastly fits of rage had I learned this skill. Sometimes, some people wanted to feel like their life was some sort of melodramatic play and upon this they thrive. This tedious quality was one shared by both Aunt Ruth and her late sister, my mother. It was best to just allow the scene to play out, to read the lines as she wanted and fulfill whatever preselected role I had been cast into.

She stood up and hugged me. The fabric of the jumper was scratchy and smelled like the police and memories flooded back.

The days after my mother's accident, as it was called, when I all but lived in those wretched places. Stark walls and white lights which hissed with the effort of persisting. Hot chocolate so weak that my mother would have called it "gnat's piss." The silence of the place only served to amplify the crack of my mother's skull on the sink basin. It rang through each room and came to me with any sudden noise. When of an evening I could feel myself slipping away into sleep, that sound would come to me again and I would bolt awake.

Swallowing down the bitter taste of those days, I put my arms around Ruth in kind. I believe that I did then hide my revulsion well. In those last few days she had clearly been forced to eat and though she was still tiny in my arms I could feel some health returning to her.

'I'm going to really try, Jacob, I am. I need to be a better version of myself. I need to do it for my children, for you. I love you, Jacob, and I am so sorry for everything. Not just what I did but everything you've gone through. It isn't fair. I don't want to be just someone else who's let you down. You've survived so much. What happened to Anne, what your father did to you. It's all too terrible for one so young. I'm so sorry. There's something extraordinary about you. Something others should fear and I *do*, I am afraid of you, but in a good way. I don't know, I can't explain it. You've survived so much and sacrificed so much of yourself.'

All this fell out of her in a barrage like vomit. I did not miss her constant talking. After releasing myself from the hug I sat down at the head of the table, bile rising in my throat as I became aware of the hot, wet patch spreading over my shoulder. The smell of it was foul.

'I'm proud of you, Jacob.'

That felt like a punch in the teeth. I could not remember if anyone had ever said that to me. Suddenly I knew it was all I had ever wanted to hear. The smile on my face and the tears in my eyes almost felt real. Or at least they may have been until Ruth saw them and started sobbing again. The sensation was akin to losing a sneeze.

'Jacob, I need to tell you something,' I inhaled deeply to beat back the surging irritation. By then I was quite tired and did not know if I had the energy for another of Ruth's confessions. The last of them haunted me still. I had found myself wondering just how insane Ruth actually was. Could the child be out there? Could it have survived somehow, raised by a vixen? There are always rumours of such things, but I had never thought them to be myths with much credence. 'I need to say it because I never have. I think once I've said it I will be better, or at least on the right path to be. I really think it will help, I think. Please, just listen.'

I knew what she was going to tell me.

'I killed your Uncle Harvey.' She said, her voice broken through tears. 'I shot him in that room that night, not him. Not him, he did not kill himself like I told everyone. He was a bastard. He was always a bastard. He made a fool of me. He fucked anyone all over town and was brazen about it. He beat me bloody dozens of times before the children came. I thought it would stop when we had Charlotte and it did, for a time. I thought we were falling in love again. Then we had Ellis.

'It was a horrible pregnancy. I was constantly in pain and I could barely eat. He did not feel the same way Charlotte did, he felt *sharper*. You don't know what I mean and I suppose I don't either but that's the truth of it. Harvey was supportive enough, but his idea of support was taking Charlotte on trips and days out so they did not have to suffer me. But it was *me* who was suffering. It was *me* who had to be with that *creature* all the time!' She covered her mouth quickly with one hand, surprised at the honesty falling out of her then. Her eyes cast down to the table after a moment and the hand slipped away as she righted herself to continue.

'When Ellis was born, Harvey blamed me for what he was. As he got older and stranger Harvey removed himself more and more. Still he was taking Charlotte away from me and I knew he was taking her with him to meet his mistresses. I could not stand that, him taking my daughter and leaving her somewhere whilst he *fucked* some other whore. He was planning on leaving me. I love Ellis, so much, I always did, even after that incident in school where I knew he was not right. But I could not handle him alone. I just knew I was not strong enough.

'I spent nights begging with Harvey to love me and then he started hitting me again. Bastard. There were times I thought about all the ways I could kill him and how to best make it look like an accident. At night I would lay there for hours, staring up into the dark of the room above me, thinking about strangling him or cutting the breaks on his car or poisoning his dinner. I thought about it a lot more on the nights when he was not there with him. Something about his presence on the other nights seemed to weaken my resolve. It was like he was worse in my memory, or maybe he saw what I was thinking and wanted to lessen my anger. I don't know, he was insidious like that. Of course there are plenty of ways to kill someone when you live in the country, out on a farm. I was going to go on a family walk, send the kids to play in a field and break his leg. It would not be all that hard to hoist his body up a tree and throw it down again, I worked out how to make a pulley system with ropes and hooks and knots. Things like that, you know? I knew I could play the grieving widow well enough.

'Of course, I never thought I would *actually* do it. Not until the day when he hit Charlotte. I could not stand it after that. I made my decision as soon as her teeth hit the floor, so little and bloody.' Again, Ruth took a shuddering breath. I had not been looking at her directly and had not known that she had been crying in the first place. Snot fell out of her left nostril and her mouth was twisted in a horribly contorted impression of abject terror.

'Really, I could not believe I got away with it. My fingerprints were everywhere, though I suppose it was my house too. I certainly had the motive and then there's the ergonomics of firing a shotgun into your own mouth. I must have been the prime suspect in any sort of enquiry, but they never told me that the death was treated as suspicious.'

'Wow,' I said after a few excruciating moments. Certainly her confession had torn my attention away from the situation with Ellis and indeed even Ruth's attack on myself and Stanley. Studying her face there was a lightness, a freedom I had not yet seen from her in any genuine way. I had not thought her capable of it, even with such justification. Looking at her then, I found there to be a whole new woman before me. No longer did I see the eccentric and unstable and yet largely harmless aunt I had known until a few days ago, but a woman scorned and a woman freed.

'I feel better.' She said. She was not crying. 'Say, where's the dog?'

I had not meant to kill the Pederson boy but he had intruded upon the birthing of my greatest piece yet.

Whilst my fingers had worked under the skin of the old bitch, separating it from the organs and muscle and gore beneath, he had come upon me. I had thought the location I had taken her to those days before had been secluded enough, but unfortunately I was erroneous. I had killed her days before and left her body there but I had felt she deserved more of a theatre, a display deserving of her status, of her significance. The boy had come upon the spot where I had worked in the low light of the evening as it was born.

He had yelled and screamed, afraid and furious. I think he had not fully been able to comprehend what it was he was looking upon. Even in that form wherein I was not quite the self he had known he saw me. I had looked to him with feral eyes and bloody hands, matching his shock.

The guttural noise that had escaped me was one conjured up from my latest victim, it had seemed and I had had to do it. I had felt that primal and aggressive part of her nature becoming part of myself as I had taken her life.

Once it was over and his body had stopped twitching as the last life had fallen away from him I stood over the mess I had made. His kind face was broken on the ground, nearly unrecognisable as the young man he had been. I would have to get back to the old bitch later. Disguising what had happened here was foremost in my mind.

Regret sickened me. I dropped the rock I had used to smash his skull into the ground where it rested, wet and dirtied by the sodden ground.

It was a shame. I did not like killing him. I did not like killing people at all. He had always been good to me, the Pederson boy.

I crouched over his body and howled my convoluted disdain.

Poor, poor, poor fellow.

More unfortunate still was the second intruder unto that dire scene. It was as though someone had wanted me to succeed in my deception and offered me a devilishly twisted gift. I had spun about with a snarl, aware then that I must have given them quite the fright in my naked and bloody visage.

They looked upon me with startled eyes which did dart between myself and the half-skinned hound and the body which no longer had a face.

Afraid of me, he made no move as I lunged towards that wayward soul.

IX

A depression hung over Crawbeth House the next day. Dark clouds were creeping in from the north bringing with them cold winds and icy rain.

Aunt Ruth was fearing another storm, but I thought that these particular dark masses looked not nearly as violent as those ones a few months before had appeared.

Chuck, Ruth, and I gathered in the kitchen nervously. Stanley had still not arrived. Ellis had been missing for more than a day and Adah seemed to have vanished as well. Try as I might, I could not calm Ruth nor Chuck. I assured them that Adah was old and afraid, the commotion of the last week had likely terrified her and she had gone to hide nearby. Deaf and blind, she could not hear our calls and was likely just confused.

The reunion of mother and daughter had been entirely without joy or love. I even saw no trace of forgiveness from either of them. Ruth had looked up with eyes magnified by tears as her daughter had come into the room shortly after she had arrived home at Crawbeth. She had looked down quickly and that salty liquid had fallen to stain upon the table. Chuck had stopped for half a heartbeat and in her own eyes I had seen a fire which paired neatly with the tightening of her jaw. Chuck plainly forgot her own guilt which had hitherto evoked a mournful air about her. Regardless of her own negligence of her younger brother, her mother's was tenfold.

To my complete lack of surprise, Ruth had taken the news that Ellis was missing with a nearly relieved calm. Still she relied on Stanley, trusted that he would be back as soon as he could with a group to help us search. Chuck tried the phone again and again but still the reception was dubious at best and nonexistent at worst. She tried the police over and over, and Stanley a few times more but with no success. All we could do was wait.

I had told them that I would be somewhat shocked if Stanley would return at all. He had had a hard time of it at Crawbeth House of late. Ruth wasted no time in reminding me pointedly that we all had. I said nothing else.

My stomach did lurch to think of Stanley. It was curious to feel something as genuine as that most violent guilt.

To my own hands I looked. The palms were dirtied still, bloodied from the rock I had wielded over poor Stanley.

My fingernails, black with filth, bit into my palms as I squeezed my eyes shut to silence the beast within. It thrashed against its chains and bellowed out hungry shrieks. It did not feel right what it had done, using my body as its instrument to do so. It had acted so primally, like a cornered animal, like that cow all those weeks ago in the barn. It had shrank away, roared even as though it knew those within, not even all that far away, could come quickly to its aid.

Few words were spoken between any of us. It suited me just fine. Without the buffer of either of the boys to add to an atmosphere, Aunt Ruth and Chuck did not say a thing to one another. The silence was pleasant. It allowed me to think.

Regardless of their protests I demanded that they ate. I made simple sandwiches of cheese and pickle which they both hungrily accepted.

Even as she ate, Ruth paced the kitchen, occasionally making an attempt to wipe a surface or dust a shelf but always without making any real progress. Her restlessness was fostering an anxiety in Chuck and I grew quite bored of it all. Before long, the kitchen was in a worse state than it had been when she had begun with cloths and cleaning bottles strewn about.

'I want my dog,' Ruth would occasionally say to the room and then carry on with whatever else she thought to busy herself with. I found it odd she did not mention Ellis, though I knew Chuck shared not in my curiosity. She knew her mother feared the boy and it was quite understandable.

He was a mad and unbroken thing, and with Ruth's limited mental capabilities I found myself impressed that she had only over those last few years started to break. Despite Ruth's confession to me that Chuck's demonising accusations of her mother were correct, I still thought her disregard of her missing and challenged son to be callous and perverse.

It was the nature of familial disasters, I suppose, that we all lingered together waiting for something, for some pain to recede or some answer to be given. I felt as though it should be Ruth to give us the direction we sorely needed, but she offered none. Perhaps she thought I would take the role of the adult, or her domineering daughter, even.

The silence, the pain, in any other family it may have been almost comforting and could cause some sort of bonding between us all. But the Dunworth family was anything but normal. Of course there would be no miraculous aid for us and all we could do was wait.

And so we did. For hours and hours with nothing changing. The sky became quite spectacular with pinks and reds and purples in the late afternoon as the heavy dark clouds passed over us, never making good on their grumbling threats. The sun shooting its fingers through the heavens became quite a serene and stupendous sight, one that I revelled in even if my companions did not.

At last we heard the back door open. It did not close. Heavy footsteps came down the hall with an even, clumping pace. Ruth righted herself then, standing awkwardly by the sink and then changing to lean on the table. She was not comfortable.

'Finally,' Chuck said, moving from the chair where she had been sitting for several hours and going to the door, 'Stanley? What took you so...' She did not finish the sentence.

I looked up from the book I had been reading to see Chuck first of all. Her eyes were wide and her mouth was locked in a silent scream. She looked as though she was made of wax, poorly formed and melting. In my life I do not think I had seen a person so utterly the perfection of terror as I did then.

Then I saw what had petrified her thusly.

Shamefully I admit I rose from my seat with some force and backed away. The chair clattered down to the floor behind me and I thought it might have broken. It took my mind a moment to really understand what it was seeing, for the scene in the hallway leading to the back door was one most foul. It was the most horrific thing, and something so dread I had not thought to ever see.

That was how I made it appear.

Ellis had returned to us after being missing for over two days. Such was the amount of time when the authorities would ordinarily turn their attention to searching for a body, I knew, but there he was, alive and well, naked, and covered in blood.

His patchy hair clung to his skin in grotesque strands thick and dark with vile viscera. His skin was hardly visible under that entire coating of horror. Bloody footprints followed him all the way up the hall to where he then stood in the kitchen doorway as though he had, until only moments prior, been dancing in some ghoulish red puddle. Those ordinarily downturned and suspicious eyes were wide and alert, his head not downcast but matching all of us, his shoulders righted and his posture nearly proud - or perhaps rigid in fright. His eyes shot about the room and between all of us rapidly as though he were in some waking dream.

He muttered under his breath in a voice which broke and squeaked with sobs and jagged breaths. None of us could hear him, nor did we try to listen to the words he said.

In his hands he held the head of a dog. It had no skin.

He held it aloft and screamed. The tendons in his neck pressed hard against his inhuman and unholy flesh.

Ellis screamed and screamed and screamed.

I could hear his throat tearing from the strain of that constant noise. Teeth gritted for moments between each long and loud breath, as though he struggled under some massive weight or strain. Then he would scream again and on and on and on it went.

The head he dropped then as he collapsed, fetal and shaking and humming.

All the air was out of the room which spun like a centrifuge. In that silence we could at last hear his voice as he uttered one word over and over and over.

'Adah. Adah. Adah. Adah. Adah. Adah. Adah...'

I acted quickly and with little active thought.

With a blanket which had been over the back of one of the chairs I leapt through the hall and enveloped Ellis.

He was the killer, everyone knew that now. Looking back it would all become so apparent. His foibles and his violence and his near animal nature. They would kick themselves for not having seen it before. He had a known history of violence. He would never be able to tell them anything otherwise to defend himself.

They would find Stanley, what was left of poor Stanley, and piece it all together seamlessly.

In my arms as I hoisted him up I found he was light as one half his age. Much of the blood which covered him had dried though not all and I felt the cool wetness slowly covering my hands and wrists, seeping through the blanket which divided us.

With a swift and thoughtless throw, I did deposit him into the side room off of the kitchen and lock the door from without. He began to scream again from within, shaking at the door handle and hammering on the door with a speed I had not thought a human might possess. After a few heartbeats of this (ones which passed with some urgency,) I ushered my aunt and Chuck out of the kitchen and closed the door behind us in a similar manner.

The dog's head still lay there, upturned in the hallway. The tongue hung limp with crystalline eyes gazing into seperate directions. We pushed passed and I shoved them both into Chuck's painting room, the room wherein Ruth had killed her husband. Ruth fell into the room, raising herself on her hands and heaving up nothing but air from her sickened gut.

I held my hands to the door as I shut it and felt a smile, one quite genuine indeed, pull at the corners of my mouth. Everything had happened as though by some divine design rather than my own hopeful planning.

Images of Ellis, some as he was and some as he was not, stared down at us. Ruth began to sob, curling herself into a ball on the floor and rocking back and forth with each crashing wave of despair.

To my surprise, Chuck lowered herself onto her mother and stretched her arms around her, weeping in tandem with her and soothing her through a disparaged voice all at once. I found it astounding that this horrid revelation could bring these two clashing people together in solidarity. Only I stood in the centre of the room, staring up at dozens of sets of Ellis' eyes looking out horrified and horribly from the canvases.

We stayed in there for hours. I went to the phone on the broken telephone table by the front door, not wanting at all to use the one in the sideroom and be faced with Ellis' wild fury.

While the police made their way to us with apparent haste, we did little. After a few hours Ruth stopped crying. She sat against the wall by the door with her mouth hanging slack and to the side, her hands limp beside her. She looked like some deflated doll.

Chuck had seemed like she had decided to paint but rather sat before her easel, looking into the white of the blank canvas like it was a television set. Her face was devoid of anything, though it was slick with tears, a curious sight upon her ordinarily stoic character.

"Where the *fuck* is Stanley?" Chuck rasped.

I did not do anything but lay on the floor, Chuck dividing me from Ruth. I stared at the ceiling and waited in the stillness and the silence for the police to arrive. I lay there, staring and thinking and trying not to smile.

I remembered the night my mother had died. I remembered how easy it had all been to disguise what I had done, just as it was in that moment in Chuck's studio. Those same flavours of victory I could feel rushing through my body then like the aftershocks of an orgasm, the kind that blinds you for a moment.

I had been too young for them to pay any attention to me. Never once had I complained about her and her ongoing abuses to anyone, neither friends nor authority figures. She had been so drunk that night that it could be ruled as nothing but an accident. Found in a towel upon a wet floor, her skull caved in matching the damage to the sink. It was all too perfect to be anything but.

Once she had been drunk enough that she would be agreeable to anything presented to her, I told her to shower. She had been crying on the floor, her speech thick and incomprehensible and her eyes hardly open, as though she was half dead already. After slapping me hard around the face earlier that evening, the devil in her eyes and the bottle in her hand which I had been trying to remove, I had made my decision, just as Ruth had done when she had seen Chuck's little teeth bounce across the floor.

For years I had known I would do it. It was just a matter of when. In the end, it had only taken a simple shove.

Such was why I had found myself so amiable to Ruth's confession of murdering her husband, my Uncle Harvey. I understood entirely just why she had done so. Why she had felt she had had no choice.

Taking her life, Ruth taking his, it was all for the safety of ourselves, those of us who were left and did not deserve what was happening to us.

We did not deserve what was happening to us.

I did not deserve what my life had become.

That putrid excuse for a mother, for a human being, and that vile man who had driven his wife to become the raving loon, talking to ghosts and scared of her own children, they did not deserve life. The world was better off, I knew.

Often I would ponder on who I might have been had I not been so afraid of the one person I should never have been.

Would I be smarter?

Would I be kind?

Would I be calmer?

Would I be happy?

If all these things and more I could have become, I would not have been myself, the unfeeling and impatient thing I was. A creature repulsed by human skin and unable to know ought but malice and anger. This I did not think in mourning, for there was no need to grieve for what was not, what would never be.

I do not know if i believe that.

I called for help at eight o'clock in the morning. The timing was believable as it was when one my age would be readying themself for the school day. They had told me to wait and I did, sitting by the body with a soft smile on my face. Occasionally I would laugh, the reality of the situation too absurd for me to believe fully but the beauty of it too tranquil to deny.

In all my life, I do not know if I had ever felt such a sense of release and achievement.

What I had not accounted for, was what might become of me after the fact. Regardless of my fantasy of the outcome, I had been driven wholly by impulse during the act itself.

Now that she was dead, my next of kin became my estranged father. He had left my mother several years before because of her alcoholism and I had heard nothing from him since due to her having severed all ties with the man.

For many years she had been pouring poison into my ear of a man I did not know. Whatever vile things he did or did not do did not matter to me. Besides, I knew how my mother was prone to lie. He had made her life painful and difficult at least, but I had no real memory of him or his behaviour towards either one of us. I preferred that unsureness to the definite horror I had faced thus far within my childhood.

He lived far away in the city and in just a few evenings my life did change utterly.

We did not know each other but there was a desperate need for familial connection from him. I did not reciprocate the desire and after some time found it infuriating. He was a stuttering and shy man, one whose attempts at connection and conversation I had to refute and deny too many times for me to count.

It became increasingly apparent that the stories my mother had spun about him had been just that. In her madness, affected largely by their separation, she had done all in her power to keep us apart. She had moved us far away and forbade any one of her family from contacting him with information as to our wearabouts.

For the first month there it had been easy enough to avoid him, utilising the guise of my fabricated grief but then he began becoming more persistent. At times I thought I had made him cry with my desire to isolate myself. It annoyed me.

He enrolled me in a local school, and little to my surprise, I loathed the place. Academically I excelled beyond the other students' capabilities. Thus I spent much time focusing on my study of the emotions of those who might have been my peer group.

I found them rash and quick to temper, but also loud with a desire to be noticed above all others. There was the fear which came alongside adolescents about every one of them which made me cringe. Many classes and breaktimess did I spend practicing mimicking their facial expressions, the flutter of their eyes as they smiled and the trembling of their brows as they cried. I repeated these to myself whenever presented with a mirror and spent many an evening echoing the behavior of my classmates to myself alone in my bedroom. It was a performance.

Always had I been told that I was different, cold and serious, even as an infant. When I had entered secondary school, I was tested for autism, though that had appeared to not be the case. In my mother's negligence, she had never pursued any other causes or treatments for my difficult personality and from then, as puberty began to change my body and mind, I found that that darkness did fester and build.

I thought about killing my father too. I could not use the same method as I had to dispatch my violent drunkard of a mother for suspicions would surely arise. Of course, they would regardless of the means I used so I would have to be more cunning.

The urge to kill was not one that I felt, in truth. My lack of caring about any other individual drove me not into a murderous berzerk but instead plateaued at indifference. At that point, my mother had been the first and last thing I had killed. I wanted to be rid of my father, certainly, but I would have to be more sly if I were to do so.

It was easy enough to go to the school counsellor and ask for help. I utilised the nights of practicing human expressions and emotions within the mirror and put on the best show I possibly could. 'Please help me.' I would say, 'I am afraid, please help me, my father has been touching me.'

Everything happened fairly quickly from there. I had to give a few statements and photographs were taken of the bruises on my body, (they had not been difficult to fake for I had always bruised quite easily.) The trial had been brief and I had found the judicial system laughable. There were massive holes in my story but the weapon I had used to rid myself of him had proven a most proficient one.

Not too many details were asked of me, nor was I pressed to give more. They all believed that I was a traumatised child, affected so deeply by the untimely demise of my mother and the most foul betrayal of my father. I suppose that they did not think it appropriate to force me to dwell on such things when there had been such an undeniable plethora of evidence against him.

Only once I had arrived at Crawbeth House had the desire to kill really manifested. Perhaps it was the silence and freedom from the city and the watchful eyes which came with it. Perhaps it was the mounting ire of my troubled life, though I find that excuse to be unremarkable and irresponsible.

Knowing I could not harm those around me for fear of discovery I turned to the most defenceless and plentiful group one might find in countryside farming communities. Animals died violent deaths all the time, I knew, and no one cared. I had to be careful to stay away from dogs and cats and other household pets for they would simply attract too much attention. Besides which, I had the echoes of love for Adah within my own soul from childhood with her. I would only turn upon her later when she had offered herself to me so readily. It had been like fate, like God had willed it and I had obliged.

For a time I had gone unnoticed, but as the villagers had realised that it was no fox or badger nor legendary hound which did the killings I knew I had to create a scapegoat.

Ruth Dunworth's ludicrous belief that her long abandoned son was responsible for the carnage which crept over the country would also not serve, particularly not when I discovered her poor reputation within the village. Fortunately, one such character existed right there in Crawbeth House.

Killing the dog had been regrettable but perhaps the most satisfactory of all. I had strung up the corpse in the woods and rubbed my frail and mindless cousin against it when he had come upon me, shortly after I had been forced to kill the Penderson boy. Ellis had hardly seemed to notice as I had smeared him in viscera, he had been too distracted by Stanley's body laying there on the stones.

Stanley I had not intended, as I have previously stated, but if he had said a word it would have caused an explosion I could not have contained.

I had liked Stanley, so it was indeed a pity. Our sex had been satisfying physically but had done nothing to soften my distant world view. He had seemed to fall very much for me in that short time after the fact and yet even that would not have prevented him from revealing my work to the authorities.

In there end, there was no choice. He had tried to leave me there in the woods with Adah's body and so he had not been aware of my picking up of the large rock which I would then use to kill him.

I knew Ellis would be able to find his way back to Crawbeth, it was just a matter of how long it would take him to do so. Regardless, when eventually he came back into the house, the effect would be the same.

When he had wandered down the hallway, things could not have been more perfect. Ruth had needed almost no convincing that it was her son who did those terrible deeds. Always had she thought him a twisted and sordid beast. With her disturbed personality, she would become easily convinced that she had seen dozens of indications, would likely even testify as much.

Chuck too would be unable to deny the apparent truth, so fragrant was it. She knew her brother was disturbed and different and the idea of him being responsible for all of that would be too believable for her to deny. She would likely think that Ellis being away somewhere

The police were on their way to us. We all saw what happened. He's a monster. He's feral. He's the one, officer, it was Ellis who did it all.

I lay there on the floor, smiling, surrounded by my catatonic family.

At last, the house would be peaceful and silent.

THE END